"You don't intimidate me, Vieri."

"No?" His gaze deliberately burned into Harper's, the small space between them humming with his threat.

"Oh, you would love that, wouldn't you?" Still she pushed. "For me to be scared of you."

"On the contrary." Reaching forward, he brushed his fingers along her jawline, before curling his hand possessively under her chin. "What I would love would be for you to honor the clearly laid-out terms of our agreement and start behaving like my fiancée."

"But..." His finger pressed against her lips to silence her.

"What I would *really* love would be for you to start showing me some respect."

Harper swallowed against her closing throat. The heat of his fingers was setting her face alight, her heart hammering wildly in her chest. In theory she only had to turn her head to release his grip, but somehow she couldn't do it. His punishing gaze was holding her captive, and it was as much as she could do to drag in a ragged breath.

"I will start showing you some respect when I think you have earned it." Somehow she managed to choke out some words.

"Is that right?" With a cold laugh Vieri moved his body fractionally closer. "So tell me, just for argument's sake, what exactly *do* I have to do to earn your respect?"

Andie Brock started inventing imaginary friends around the age of four and is still doing that today—only now the sparkly fairies have made way for spirited heroines and sexy heroes. Thankfully, she now has some real friends, as well as a husband and three children, plus a grumpy but lovable cat. Andie lives in Bristol, and when not actually writing might well be plotting her next passionate romance story.

Books by Andie Brock

Harlequin Presents

The Last Heir of Monterrato

Secret Heirs of Billionaires
The Greek's Pleasurable Revenge

Wedlocked!
Bound by His Desert Diamond

One Night With Consequences
The Shock Cassano Baby

Society Weddings
The Sheikh's Wedding Contract

Visit the Author Profile page
at Harlequin.com for more titles.

Andie Brock

———

VIERI'S CONVENIENT VOWS

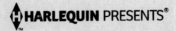

Recycling programs
for this product may
not exist in your area.

ISBN-13: 978-1-335-50426-5

Vieri's Convenient Vows

First North American publication 2018

Copyright © 2018 by Andrea Brock

This edition published by arrangement with Harlequin Books S.A.

For questions and comments about the quality of this book, please contact us at CustomerService@Harlequin.com.

Printed in U.S.A.

www.Harlequin.com

VIERI'S CONVENIENT VOWS

For my sisters, Linda, Jo and Diana.
Love you loads. xxx

CHAPTER ONE

HARPER MCDONALD GAZED at the mass of bodies writhing on the dance floor. With green and blue laser lights playing over their jerky movements they somehow produced a mesmerising whole, like a choppy sea. A DJ was performing on the elevated stage, the pulsing music so invasive that Harper could feel it reverberating through her body, defying her to stand still. She had never witnessed anything so hedonistic, so tribal. Even the air felt different, heavy with the scent of luxury and indulgence and wealth.

As another impossibly glamorous couple swept past her, Harper pulled in a breath, trying to ignore the way her stomach was knotting inside her. She felt so out of place she might as well have had a pair of antlers on her head. But she wasn't here to blend in or to dance or to schmooze with the beautiful people. She was here for one reason only. To find her sister.

Descending the stairs, she tentatively started

to skirt the edge of the dance floor, looking for someone who might be able to help her. Somebody here had to have some information, had to know what had happened to Leah. But she had only gone a few steps when she was physically halted. With a shriek of terror she found herself airborne, both arms grabbed in a vice-like grip, the hold so powerful that her feet were lifted clean off the ground.

'Get off me! Put me down!' Frantically turning her head, she saw a pair of giant, suited men, their wide, impassive faces eerily shadowed by the coloured lights, giving nothing away. With a surge of adrenaline she tried to twist inside their grasp but this only made their brutish hands tighten further. Panic washed over her.

'I insist that you put me down.' She tried again, raising her voice over the incessant throb of noise, kicking her legs beneath her. 'You're hurting me.'

'Then stop squirmin'.'

Offering no more than this one piece of advice, the pair of man beasts continued to move forward, Harper trapped between them like the filling of a sandwich. The crowd of revellers parted to let them through with surprisingly little interest in her plight. No one seemed remotely interested in helping her.

'Stop this!' She battled to halt the hysteria that was rising in her throat. She didn't have a clue who these thugs were, only that she was being forcibly escorted against her will. And not even towards the entrance where the idea of being evicted into the chill of the night suddenly seemed all too inviting. No, she was being propelled in the opposite direction, further into the mysterious depths of this dark and dangerous place. A series of terrifying images flashed through her mind— abduction, murder, rape. And then the worst dread of all—was this what had happened to Leah?

Well, there was no way she would let herself be taken. She would fight with everything she had to save herself and her sister. 'I'm warning you.' She kicked her legs wildly beneath her once more. 'If you don't put me down right now I will scream so loud I will burst your eardrums.'

'I wouldn't advise that,' a low voice growled in her ear. 'If I were you I'd keep nice an' quiet. When you've done what you've done you've gotta expect consequences. Makin' a fuss ain't gonna help nothing.'

Done? What had she done? Surely they weren't talking about her fooling the security at the door?

Gaining entrance to this exclusive, members' only nightclub had proved to be surprisingly easy. Sidling up to the bouncer, she had been prepared for trouble, deciding she would have to throw herself on his mercy and explain why she was here. But no explanation had been necessary. The guy had moved aside and waved her straight in, uttering, 'Nice of you to join us again,' in a deep, mocking voice. Because of course he had thought she was her sister. He had thought she was Leah.

The last Harper had heard from her twin had been over a month ago, a drunken phone call in the wee small hours, Leah never having had any respect for the time difference between Scotland and New York. Harper's sleep-fuddled brain had struggled to understand what Leah was telling her—something about having met a man who was going to make her rich, how the family would never have to worry about money again.

And then nothing. As time had gone on the creeping concern that something was wrong had quickly escalated into a full-blown panic that a dreadful fate must have befallen her sister. Enough to see Harper maxing out her credit card to fly to New York and make her way to this alien venue, deep in the heart of Manhattan. Spectrum nightclub, where Leah had been working as a hostess since she'd left their home in Scotland six months ago. The last place she had been seen before she had disappeared and the only place Harper could think of to start looking for her.

Now, as she was physically propelled forward by these fearsome man beasts towards God knew what end, Harper couldn't help but panic that in coming to try and save her sister, she was about to suffer the same unknown fate.

At the back of the club, she found herself being bundled through a concealed door behind the stage and into a dark passageway. It was so narrow that the trio had to go in single file, her minders finally letting go of her arms but positioning themselves in front of and behind her, so close that she could feel the heat coming off them, smell the sweat. They ascended a dimly lit flight of stairs until they reached a door at the top and they moved beside her again. One of them rapped his knuckles against the matte black paint.

'Enter.'

Harper was shoved into a small, square office, lit by a single florescent strip light. A dark-haired man sat at a desk facing the door, his head bent, his fingers rapidly tapping at the keys of a computer. Behind him, a long rectangle of glass, a two-way mirror, gave an uninterrupted view of the undulating mass below.

'Thanks, guys.' Still he didn't look up. Harper noticed the way the light shone blue-black on the thick waves of his hair. 'You may go.'

With subservient grunts the pair shuffled out, closing the door behind them.

Harper desperately tried to steady her heart rate, to think clearly. Her eyes flitted around the room to see if there was any means of escape. It was almost totally silent in here, she realised. The pulsating beat that had been with her ever since she had entered the nightclub had gone, replaced by the roaring of blood in her ears and the gentle tap of the laptop keyboard.

She stared at the man before her. Even though he was seated and steadfastly ignoring her, she could sense the power of him. But there was something else, something worse, an enmity that was radiating from him like a palpable force. Suddenly being left alone with this silent, formidable figure was worse than being manhandled by those gorillas. She was almost tempted to run after them, ask them to take her with them.

'So.' Still he refused to look at her. 'The wanderer returns.'

'No!' With a rush of breath, Harper hurried to put him right. 'You don't understand…'

'Spare me the excuses.' Finally closing his laptop, the dark figure rose gracefully to his feet and Harper realised with a gulp how tall he was, how handsome, how effortlessly cool. 'I'm really not interested.' Still refusing to look her in the eye, he strolled casually to the door behind her. She heard him turn a key in the lock before slipping the key into his trouser pocket as he returned to his desk.

'W…what are you doing?'

'What does it look like I'm doing?' He stood

by his seat. 'I'm making sure you don't escape. Again.'

'No.' Harper tried again. 'You're making a mistake. I'm not—'

'Sit down.' He barked the order, gesturing to the chair opposite his. 'There is no point in making this any harder than it already is.'

Harper edged forward and did as she was told. She felt as if she had fallen into some sort of rabbit hole. That none of this was real.

Seating himself, her captor folded his arms across his chest, his eyes finally meeting hers for the first time. And only then did his icy composure slip.

Che diavolo? What the hell? Vieri Romano ground down on his jaw. *It was the wrong damned woman!* A surge of frustration went through him as he clenched his fists. The person before him looked like Leah McDonald and she sounded like Leah McDonald, with that soft, lilting Scottish accent. But now that he was glaring at her beneath the harsh overhead light he knew with irritating certainty that she was *not* Leah McDonald.

Hell. He raked a hand through his hair as he continued to stare at this imposter. They were certainly very alike, obviously twins, but the subtle differences were now clear to see. This young woman's eyes were wider apart, the lips fuller, the nose a tad longer. Her hair was different too, falling in careless auburn waves compared to Leah's more styled tresses. But even without these differences, Vieri would have known this wasn't Leah, simply by her manner.

The woman before him was all serious determination. There was no sign of Leah's flirty confidence—something that Vieri suspected Leah would be trying to use right now to get herself out of trouble, had he managed to get the correct sister in front of him. Leah was well aware of her assets and knew how to use them, whereas her sister appeared uncomfortable beneath his scrutiny, wrapping her arms around herself to cover up her slender but shapely figure. And if Leah's eyes would have been batting seductively by now, her sister's glared at him, full of fire. She reminded Vieri of a cornered animal, one that was most definitely not going to give up without a fight.

But then neither did he. Vieri ran a hand over his jaw, rapidly assessing this new situation. Maybe they were in it together, this pair of Celtic beauties. He wouldn't put it past them. Perhaps this one had been sent as backup. They might just be dumb enough to think they could get away with it. Although dumb was not a word he would use to describe the woman sitting across from him now. There was something about her that suggested a sharp intelligence. If nothing else, it was possible she might be able to lead him to her double-crossing sister. One thing was for sure, she wouldn't be leaving here until she had been thoroughly interrogated.

'Name?' He barked the question at her.

'Harper.' She shifted in her seat. 'Harper Mc-Donald.'

When he didn't immediately reply she tipped her chin in a show of defiance. 'And you are?'

Vieri's brows snapped together. He wasn't accustomed to being asked who he was. Least of all in one of his own establishments.

'Vieri Romano.' He kept his tone steady. 'Owner of Spectrum nightclub.'

'Oh.' He watched her full pink lips purse closed as realisation dawned. 'Then I should like to formally complain about the way I have been treated here. You have absolutely no right to—'

'Where is your sister, Ms McDonald?' Raising his voice, Vieri cut short her futile protests. He had no time to listen to her pathetic accusations.

She bit down on her lip, nipping the soft flesh with her front teeth, the action engaging Vieri more than it should. 'I don't know.' He could hear the panic in her voice. 'That's why I'm here, to try and find her. I haven't heard from her in over a month.'

Pulling his eyes away from her seductive

mouth, Vieri let out a derisive grunt. 'Well, that makes two of us.'

'So she's not here?' The panic escalated. 'She quit her job?'

'She has walked out, if that's what you mean. Along with my bar manager, Max Rodriguez.'

'Walked out?'

'*Si*. Disappeared without a trace.'

'Oh, God.' Harper reached forward to grip the edge of the desk with hands that visibly shook. 'Where has she gone?'

Vieri shrugged his lack of knowledge, watching her reaction closely.

'You have no idea what might have happened to her?'

'Not yet.' He picked up some papers on his desk, tidying them into a pile. 'But I intend to find out. And when I do, her troubles will be just beginning.'

'Wh…what do you mean by that?' Harper's remarkable green-brown eyes widened.

'I mean that I don't take kindly to my employees disappearing off the face of the earth. Especially with thirty thousand dollars of my money.'

'Thirty thousand dollars?' Her hands flew to her mouth. 'You mean Leah and this Max guy have stolen money from you?'

'Your sister and I had a business arrangement, or so I thought. I made the mistake of paying her the first instalment up front. She has absconded with the money.'

'No! Oh, I'm so sorry!'

She looked suitably shocked, enough to convince Vieri that she knew nothing about it, but he noted with interest that she didn't challenge the facts.

'She will be too, believe me.'

He leant back in his chair. Much as he blamed Leah for her devious deceit, most of his fury was directed at himself. How could he have been so stupid as to fall for her sob story and give her the payment in advance? All that garbage about needing the money straight away to send back home to her family, for her father who was struggling to keep his job. It smarted like a smack in the face. Not the thirty thousand dollars—he didn't give a damn about that. If she had had the guts to ask him outright for the money he might well have given it to her. But the fact was that he, Vieri Romano, billionaire businessman, international tycoon, a man both revered and feared in the corporate world, had been taken for a fool. By a woman. Something he had sworn would never happen again.

But Leah McDonald had caught him at a low point, when his defences had been down. And what had seemed like a good idea at the time, the ideal solution in fact, had now spectacularly backfired.

He had been drinking in the club one evening, uncharacteristically feeling the need to drown his sorrows after the news he had received earlier that day. Leah had been his waitress. She had been attentive but discreet, just the way he liked his staff to be. On another night he might have made a mental note to congratulate the management on their staff training. But tonight, to his surprise, he found he just wanted to talk. And so he had, sharing a quiet booth and a bottle of Scotch, appropriately enough, with this bright-eyed Scottish woman. With her soothing encouragement he had told her about his godfather, the man who meant more to Vieri than anyone else in the world. The only person who meant anything to him. How he had received an email from the man that morning, confirming Vieri's worst fears. His godfather was dying. It was just a matter of time.

Had he left it there no harm would have been done. He would have gone home to continue his drinking and Leah would have pocketed a handsome tip, just another night and another guy offloading his troubles. Even if this time the guy was the boss. But something about her gentle voice had drawn him in, made him go further, and he had found himself telling her about the last time he had seen his godfather, the heart-to-heart they had had. How Alfonso had revealed to him what he had suspected at the time and now knew for sure, his dying wish. To see Vieri settled. With a wife. A family. The one thing Vieri had never had. Nor ever would have.

And Leah's response had been remarkably practical. If that was his godfather's last wish then it had to be accomplished. It was Vieri's duty. She had been quite adamant about it. If there were no genuine contenders for the role of fiancée, then he would have to find somebody, pay someone if necessary. Anything to make his godfather happy.

And to Vieri's surprise he found himself wondering if maybe this young woman was right. Maybe that was the solution. He had always made his godfather proud, he didn't doubt that, but this was different. This was about happiness. Something that for all his wealth and success Vieri had never fully understood. But he did know that if there was any way of fulfilling his godfather's dying wish, he would give it a go. Even if it meant a bit of subterfuge.

And so, by the time he had savoured the last of the peaty whisky at the bottom of his glass, the deal had been struck. Leah needed money and he needed a fake fiancée. In return for a down payment of thirty thousand dollars, Leah would pretend to be engaged to him for a couple of months, or for as long as it took. At the time, his alcohol-soaked brain had thought it the ideal solution. A way of making his godfather happy that didn't involve messy emotions. The potentially insoluble problem had suddenly shaped into something that he could control, something he understood better than anything else—a business deal.

But that was then. No sooner had Vieri paid the money into Leah's account than she had absconded. But, crucially, not before he had announced to his delighted godfather that he had taken his advice. That his wish had been granted and Vieri would be introducing him to his fiancée in the very near future.

Now he was left with a problem. When security had alerted him that Leah was back he had made the short journey from his offices in Midtown Manhattan, determined to have it out with her, to make her honour the deal. But the defiant young woman perched on the seat before him wasn't Leah McDonald and he was no closer to solving the infuriating situation.

Or was he? Harper McDonald said she had no idea where Leah was and he believed her. But maybe she could help him in another way.

Vieri coldly assessed the twin sister in front of him, his eyes narrowing as he waited for common sense to veto the crazy idea that had popped into his mind. Because it was crazy, wasn't it?

'So what do you intend to do?' Harper's anxious voice cut through his thoughts. 'About Leah, I mean. Have you involved the police?'

'Not yet. I prefer to deal with these things in my own way. For the time being at least.' He drummed his fingers meaningfully on the desk.

It had the desired effect. He saw her swallow hard, her imagination no doubt running away with her. Well, he wasn't going to try and stop it. For the time being it would suit his purposes to let her fear him. The fact that he abhorred physical violence and had striven to eradicate any organised crime from his establishments was of no consequence.

'Look, I can help you find her.' Like a fish on a hook, Harper squirmed about, trying to come up with something that would appease him. 'And I'll pay the money back myself if I have to. All of it.'

'And how exactly will you do that?' Vieri regarded her coolly. 'From what Leah tells me, your family are destitute.'

He saw the flush creep up her neck. 'She had no right to say such a thing!'

'So it's not true? Paying back thirty thousand dollars won't be a problem?'

'Well, of course it will a problem, the same as it would be for any normal family. But that doesn't mean I won't do it.'

'Really?'

'Yes, really.' She pushed her hair away from

her heated face. 'I could work here, for example, for free, I mean.'

'I think one McDonald sister working in this establishment was more than enough, thank you.' Sarcasm scored his words.

'Well, some other job, then. I'm practical and capable and a fast learner. I'll do anything. I just need a bit of time and the chance to try and find Leah myself.'

'Anything, you say?'

'Yes.' Sheer determination was written all over her pretty face.

'In that case maybe there is something you could help me with.' He deliberately held her gaze. 'You could honour the commitment made by your sister.'

'Yes, of course.' She blinked, thick lashes sweeping low over those wide hazel eyes. 'What is it?'

A beat of silence hung in the air.

'To become my fiancée.'

CHAPTER TWO

'YOUR FIANCÉE?'

The word sounded just as ridiculous when choked from Harper's closing throat as it had done uttered from Vieri's now purposefully drawn lips.

'*Si*, that is correct.'

'You want me to marry you?'

'No.' He gave a harsh laugh. 'I can assure you it won't come to that.'

'What, then? I don't understand.'

'Your sister and I made a deal. In return for a generous payment she agreed to play the part of my fiancée for a limited period of time. It's really not that complicated.'

Not to him maybe, or her loony sister. But Harper was certainly struggling with the concept. 'But why? And what does limited mean?'

'In answer to your first question, in order to please my godfather. And as for the second, it will just be for a matter of weeks, months at the most.' He paused and took a breath. 'My godfather is dying.'

'Oh.' Harper could see the pain in Vieri's eyes. 'I'm so sorry.'

Vieri shrugged. 'His last wish is for me to settle down, take a wife, start a family. I would like to be able to fulfil that wish, in part at least.'

'But how? I mean, if it's just a lie…surely that wouldn't be right?'

'I prefer to think of it as a small deception.'

Harper frowned. It still sounded like a lie to her. 'And Leah agreed to this?' She didn't know why she was bothering to ask. It was just the sort of madcap idea that her sister would leap at.

'Actually, it was her idea.'

That figured.

'So what exactly is the deal? What did Leah sign up for?' She swallowed hard, bracing herself for the answer, a kick of dread in her stomach. Thirty thousand dollars was a huge sum of money. And had she heard him say that was the first instalment? But she knew Leah—she could have agreed to just about anything for such riches. An *anything* that Harper herself might now have to honour. It was a terrifying thought.

'Flying to Sicily, meeting my godfather, acting like the doting fiancée.'

Harper nervously chewed her fingernail, waiting for more information.

'It may entail several visits, maybe some lengthier stays. I would like to spend as much time with him as possible.'

'I see.' A tight silence fell between them as Harper tried to get to grips with this. 'Go on.'

'That's it. The arrangement between Leah and myself was left deliberately fluid.'

Deliberately fluid? What the hell did that mean? Faced with this formidably handsome man, Harper found her thoughts flying in some very surprising directions. Reining herself in, she stared at him primly. 'Obviously before I agree to anything I need to know what else would be expected of me.'

Vieri made a low noise in his throat. 'If you mean will you have to share my bed, then the answer is no.' His dark, mocking gaze slashed across her hot cheeks. 'I am not in the habit of paying women to sleep with me.'

'No, of course not.' Harper hurriedly tried to erase the erotic image of being in Vieri's bed. 'Anyway, I know my sister would never have agreed to such a thing.' That had to be true. Didn't it? 'And neither would I, to be clear.'

Argh. Why didn't she stop digging and shut up?

'I'm very pleased to hear it.' His deep blue gaze slid over her. 'So, do we have a deal? Are you prepared to take on your sister's debt?'

'I don't know.' Still Harper hesitated. 'If I did, what would happen about Leah?'

'I would have no further interest in her.'

If Harper had thought his bald statement would be a comfort, she was wrong. Suddenly the idea that Vieri Romano had lost all interest in her sister worried her almost as much as the thought of him hounding her. She didn't know how to start tracking Leah down, whereas Vieri knew people; he would have contacts, resources at his disposal.

'But what about this Rodriguez guy? You must want to speak to him?' A sudden spark of hope mixed with fear lit inside her. 'He might be the one responsible for stealing your money. He might have kidnapped Leah.'

'Unlikely. From the little I saw of your sister she didn't look like kidnap material.'

'And what exactly does *kidnap material* look like?' Harper indignantly challenged the idea that no one would want to kidnap Leah, and, by association, her too.

'Heiresses, high-profile celebrities, children of the filthy rich.'

Clearly the McDonald sisters were none of those things.

'Well, there's the thirty thousand dollars. Rodriguez might have somehow lured Leah away to try and get his hands on that.'

'Possible, though unlikely. Rodriguez has been

working as a bar manager here for some time, having access to large sums of money every night of the week. There's never been any suggestion that he's stolen from us before. My guess is that, if anything, your sister has lured him away. Though I've no idea why.'

Neither did Harper. But right now she didn't have the capacity to try and work it out.

'But you are right.' Ruthlessly, Vieri continued. 'If a member of my staff walks out with no warning, regardless of the circumstances, I make it my business to investigate. I will find Rodriguez. And if your sister is still with him, then I will see that she is returned to her family.'

'Without involving the police?'

'I see no reason to contact the police.'

'Or violence. I would hate to think anyone would get hurt.'

Rising to his feet, Vieri walked around the desk until he was standing in front of her, towering over her, all formidable dark presence.

'I think perhaps I need to make a few things clear, Ms McDonald.' He locked eyes with hers, the dark intensity of his words matched by the stark angles of his handsome face. 'I will deal with this incident as I see fit. I make the decisions. I make the rules. You should consider yourself extremely fortunate that you have this opportunity to prevent Leah from a possible prison sentence.'

Fortunate? That was not a word Harper would use to describe herself right now. Her head was spinning with the shock and sheer enormity of what was being asked of her. But what choice did she have?

'So what do you say?' Vieri fixed her with a punishing stare. 'Are you prepared to go along with my plan to save your sister's skin?'

Harper looked away, balling her hands into fists. Right now she would like to flay Leah herself, string her up and set about her, make her see what a completely stupid, totally irresponsible person she was. But Leah was her sister, her twin, almost a part of her. Of course she would save her—she would do anything to keep her safe, to protect her. It was what she had been doing the whole of their lives. Because Harper was the older twin, the sensible one, the *healthy* one. The one that shouldered the responsibility, took charge, tried to make everything right. Which in this case meant temporarily shackling herself to this shockingly attractive but coldly calculating man.

'Yes.' Her voice came out as little more than a whisper but as she raised her eyes to meet Vieri's she saw the look of satisfaction reflected in his midnight stare. Her fate had been sealed.

Harper peered through the window as the island of Sicily came into view, its iconic position off the toe of Italy's boot clearly visible from the air. As Vieri's private jet started to descend she craned her neck for a better look, taking in the rivers and the mountains, the clumps of towns and cities and, the most amazing of all, Mount Etna, shrouded in snow but puffing out a stream of smoke in welcome.

She had only ever been abroad once before, a bargain break holiday to the Costa del Sol in Spain when she was nineteen. Which might have been fun if she hadn't ended up trailing around after Leah trying to keep her out of trouble.

And nothing had changed. Here she was again, still trying to sort one of her sister's messes. But this time it was serious, really serious. Leah had stolen a large sum of money and Harper didn't doubt that if Vieri decided to press charges she could well go to prison.

Which was why she'd had no choice but to put her own life on hold and climb into Vieri's private jet to be flown back across the world to take part in this hateful little charade. She could kill Leah. She really could.

And it had all happened ridiculously fast—less than twenty-four hours had passed since she had first set foot in Spectrum nightclub. Once she had agreed to go along with the plan Vieri had leapt into action, insisting on sending a car to pick up Harper's suitcase from the hostel she had checked into earlier, refusing to even let her go with it. No doubt he was worried that if he let her out of his sight she would abscond—just like her sister. So now here she was, thousands of miles away, about to embark on a crazy deception.

It had been a long flight, starting in the small hours of the morning, and even though Harper had been shown to a sumptuous bedroom she had found sleep impossible, eventually venturing into the lounge area, where Vieri had been immersed in work, the light from the screen of his laptop suffusing his handsome face with an eerie glow. He had shown no interest in conversing with her so instead she had scrolled through the movies on the wide-screen television, in the hope of finding something to take her mind off things. Which was impossible. How was she supposed to divert herself from the mad reality of what she was doing? Pitching up with a man who was almost a total stranger and pretending to be his fiancée.

But it was happening. As the plane landed she looked across at her 'fiancé', watching as he closed his laptop, unbuckled his seat belt and drew himself up to his full height. He shrugged on a dark cashmere coat, then ushered her down the steps of the plane and across the tarmac to the waiting car.

'Castello di Trevente,' Vieri instructed the

driver once they were both seated inside, before settling back against the soft leather.

'Where are we going?' Harper addressed his strong profile.

'Castello di Trevente,' Vieri repeated. 'It's where my godfather lives.'

'He lives in a castle?' Harper's Sicilian was non-existent but even she could understand that.

'Yes, it's been in the Calleroni family for generations.' Vieri turned to look at her. 'Far too big and cold and draughty for him, of course, but Alfonso would never agree to move to anywhere more sensible.'

'I see.' Harper tucked her unruly hair behind her ears. 'But aren't we going to the hotel first, to freshen up, I mean?'

'I don't want to leave it too late. My godfather gets very tired and it's already six p.m. here.' Removing his heavy gold watch, he deftly adjusted the time before refastening it and raising his eyes to coldly assess her. In the dim light of the car his eyes flicked mercilessly over her body and Harper flinched beneath his scrutiny, tugging at the collar of her waxed jacket. Without saying a word he had managed to convey her obvious shortcomings, the world of difference between them. He oozed dark sophistication, whereas she felt as craggy and unkempt as the wild moorlands she came from.

But she refused to be intimidated by him. He might have all the wealth and power, and thanks to Leah's stupid deal it seemed he as good as owned Harper for the foreseeable future. But she still had her self-respect. And she would hang onto that for dear life.

Sitting up a little straighter, she sneaked a look at her companion. He was facing ahead again now, the collar of his coat turned up, but she could still see the dark shadow of stubble along his jaw, the loose curls of his dark hair that softened his austere profile. His hands rested in his lap, beautiful hands with long, strong fingers that invited their touch, making Harper wonder what they would feel like against her skin.

Which was ridiculous and totally uncalled for. With a jolt she put the brakes on her imagination. She and Vieri Romano had entered into a business deal, nothing more. And wondering what it would feel like to be caressed by his hands was most definitely not part of that deal. She needed to focus on the practicalities. That was what she was good at.

'So, what's the plan, then?' She broke the silence and Vieri turned to look at her, his dark brows raised. 'How am I supposed to act in front of your godfather?'

'Like my fiancée,' he replied coolly. 'I thought we had established that.'

'But shouldn't we have some sort of story mapped out?' Ever the pragmatist, she pressed on. 'How we met, how long we have known each other, that sort of thing?'

'You can leave the talking to me.'

Harper bristled. The idea that she was just going to be paraded in front of this man like some sort of inanimate object didn't sit well with her feminist principles. But then who was she kidding? None of this sat well with any of her principles. Even so, a thought occurred to her.

'Perhaps your godfather doesn't speak English?' That would explain Vieri's high-handed manner.

'Aflonso speaks perfect English.'

So that was that theory crushed. And it would make her job harder, even though Vieri didn't seem to recognise it.

'Then obviously I need to be able to converse with him.' She tried to assert some authority. 'And to do that I need to know more about him. And we need to know more about each other.' She tailed off, her authority already slipping away. Talking about herself was not a subject she was comfortable with.

'Very well.' Vieri immediately pounced on her reluctance, his full attention suddenly on her. 'Tell me your life story, Ms Harper McDonald.'

Harper swallowed hard. Her life story was not

something she was fond of recounting. Everyone in her home town of Glenruie knew it anyway—those poor wee girls, left motherless by a tragic accident that took their mother then drove their father to drink. Left struggling to make ends meet, to keep a roof over their heads. But where strangers were concerned, Harper was careful to keep her tale of woe to herself. Except now this particular stranger was silently, unnervingly waiting for answers. She decided she would stick firmly to the facts.

'Umm, well, I am twenty-five years old and I've lived all my life in a small town called Glenruie on the west coast of Scotland with my father and my sister.' She paused. 'My father is a gamekeeper for the Craigmore estate. He manages the birds and the fishing for Craigmore Lodge, which is still owned by the Laird but now run as a hotel. Leah and I work there sometimes, housekeeping, waitressing, that sort of thing.'

'And your mother?'

'She died.' Harper pursed her lips, then forced herself to continue. 'A long time ago now. An accident with a shotgun.'

'I'm sorry.' Vieri lowered his voice.

'That's okay.' But of course it wasn't. In truth the accident had all but decimated their lives.

'And I gather there are problems with your father.'

Harper silently cursed her sister again. 'Umm, he hasn't been well lately so things have been a bit tough.'

'Leah said he's a drinker.' She really would kill Leah. 'Is it true that if he loses his job you lose your home?'

'Well, in theory that could happen. But I'm sure it won't come to that. Anyway...' she folded her arms over her chest '...that's enough about me.' She attempted a small laugh that died in the purring quiet of the car. 'What should I know about you?'

Vieri laid his arm on the armrest between them, his fingers curling over the end. He turned to the front. 'Thirty-two. Sicilian by birth but I've been living in New York for fourteen years. CEO of Romano Holdings. I started in the hotel and leisure industry, but now control over a hundred companies, and that number is growing all the time.'

Harper frowned. This wasn't the sort of information she wanted. She wasn't looking to invest or compiling a list of the world's most successful businesses, though she had no doubt that if she did Romano Holdings would be up there at the top. She was supposed to be engaged to him, for heaven's sake; she was supposed to know him *personally.*

'What about your family?' She focussed on his proud profile. 'Parents, brothers and sisters?'

'No, none.' His voice was bleak, his hand tightening on the armrest.

'What, no living relatives at all?' His obvious reticence only made her want to push further.

'No.' A muscle now twitched in his cheek. 'I was raised in a children's home.'

'Oh.' The word seemed ridiculously inadequate. 'Did your parents die, then?'

'I've no idea. But if not they might as well have done. I was left on the steps of a church when I was a few hours old.'

'Oh, how sad.' The image of the tiny abandoned bundle lodged in her mind and refused to be shifted.

'Not really. I've done pretty well for myself.'

'Well, yes, of course, but—'

'And from what I've seen of other people's families, maybe I was better off without one.'

Was that a swipe at her? Harper scowled to herself.

'But actually I was very lucky. Alfonso Calleroni was a trustee of the children's home. He looked out for me, became my godfather. Without him I may well have strayed down the wrong path.'

'You owe him a lot?'

'Everything.' Harper could hear the emotion

in his voice. 'Which is why I want to do this one last thing for him. His happiness means a great deal to me.'

Harper hesitated. A thought had occurred to her that wouldn't be pushed away. 'Do you not think…' she started cautiously, all too aware that Vieri was not the sort of man who liked to be challenged '…that your godfather is thinking about *your* happiness when he says he wants to see you married? Not his own.'

Swinging round to face her again, Vieri positively shimmered with hostility. 'In the unlikely event that I should ever want your opinion, Harper McDonald, I will ask for it.' His voice was a low hiss. 'Until then I will thank you to keep your thoughts to yourself and do the job your sister has been paid to do. Is that understood?'

'Perfectly.' Harper straightened her back and turned to look out of the window. From now on she would keep her mouth shut. Even if she was the only one who could see this whole charade was stupid.

The rest of the short journey was travelled in silence until the car slowed before turning off the main road and up a long driveway. Only when it drew to a halt did Vieri turn to look at her again.

'Before we go in, you will be needing this.' Slipping his hand into his trouser pocket, he brought out a ring box and passed it to her. The velvet box was still warm from where it had nestled against his thigh. 'If it doesn't fit we can get it resized.'

Harper cautiously opened the box, realising she was holding her breath as she did so. Which was stupid. What did it matter what the ring looked like, or indeed if it was as fake as their engagement? Nevertheless as she removed it from the box, felt the weight of the green stone, saw its mocking sparkle in the dim light of the car, she had no doubt that this was the real thing. When she slid it onto her finger it fitted perfectly. Which only made her feel more uncomfortable. As did Vieri's dark gaze, which drifted from her hand to her face, making her stomach do an inexplicable swoop.

'You are ready?'

Harper nodded, stuffing the offending hand into her coat pocket to keep it from view as the driver came around to open her car door for her. 'Yes.' Somehow the right word came out, even though every part of her body was screaming no.

'*Bene*. Then let's do this.'

CHAPTER THREE

'COME A LITTLE closer so that I can see you better, *mia cara.*'

Harper did as she was told, edging towards the reclining chair where Alfonso Calleroni was propped up by a pile of cushions, a blanket draped over his bony knees.

'Ah, that's better. Sit here beside me. Vieri, don't just stand there. Pull up a chair for your young lady.'

Vieri dutifully produced a chair and placed it beside his godfather. Harper awkwardly settled herself down. If this whole situation weren't bad enough, Vieri was making it worse by standing right behind her, his hands on the back of the chair, his unnerving presence all around her.

'So, Harper, you say. Have I got that right?'

'Yes.' Harper suspected from her very brief acquaintance with Alfonso Calleroni that he probably got most things right. Despite his age and frailty and the poor state of his health she could tell he was still a very astute man. Which meant he wasn't going to be easy to fool. Only now did she realise that she had been hoping Vieri's god-father's faculties would be somewhat impaired. Which was an awful thing to hope for. Ashamed of herself, she tried to make up for her nastiness by giving him a bright smile. 'That's right.'

'And is that a Scottish name? Am I correctly attributing that wonderful accent of yours?'

'Yes.' He was as sharp as a pin. 'But the name came from my mother's favourite book, *To Kill a Mockingbird*. She called me and my twin sister Harper and Leah. As a loose sort of tribute.'

'So there are two of you? How wonderful.'

'Yes.' Although it felt slightly less wonderful from where she was sitting.

'And you met in New York, Vieri was telling me? A long way from home.'

'Harper's sister, Leah, was working in one of my clubs. Harper came to visit her,' Vieri smoothly interjected.

'And the two of you fell in love.' One gnarled, arthritic hand reached out to take hold of Harper's, holding it in his shaky grasp so that he could inspect the traitorous ring. 'How wonderful.' He raised his rheumy eyes to Harper's face. 'And your parents? I trust Vieri has done the right thing and spoken to your father to ask for your hand in marriage.'

Harper swallowed.

'Not yet, Alfonso.' Vieri cut in again. 'This has all happened rather fast. We wanted you to be the first to know.'

'Of course you did.' Alfonso's eyes travelled to Vieri's face, lingering there for several seconds. 'After all, I won't be around much longer. It would have been such a shame for me to die without knowing you had chosen a wife for yourself, wouldn't it now?'

'Let's not talk about dying, *padrino*.'

'Ah, but I am afraid we must, *mio figlio*. There are things that need to be discussed now that my time on this earth is short.' Raising Harper's hand, he brought it to his lips and gave the back of it a dry kiss. 'But I am tired now so I think they must wait for another day. Thank you so much for coming to see me, my dear.' He shifted in his seat, his face suddenly contorting with pain so that his nurse, who had been hovering in the background, rushed forward to help him. 'You have chosen well, Vieri. She is a lovely girl.'

As he pressed a button on his chair it slowly started to lever him upright until he was able to lean forward and grasp the walking frame that had been positioned in front of him by his nurse. 'Now, if you will excuse me.'

'Of course.' Vieri bent to give his godfather a kiss on the cheek. 'We will see you tomorrow.'

'Tomorrow, yes.' Alfonso gave him a weak smile. 'Let us see what tomorrow will bring.'

The next day's visit involved a longer stay, as did the day after that. Alfonso obviously delighted in his godson's company, the affection between them clear to see. But the affection between Vieri and Harper was another matter. Far from treating her like the love of his life, Vieri merely paraded her like some sort of trophy, to be perched on a chair and then ignored. With Alfonso's sharp intelligence missing nothing, Harper was becoming more and more convinced that they weren't putting on a good enough act.

On the third day, after returning to Vieri's stunning penthouse apartment in the luxury hotel he owned in Palermo, she decided she couldn't keep quiet any longer. Shrugging off her coat, she confronted Vieri.

'I'm worried that Alfonso knows we are not a real couple.'

'Why do you say that?' Vieri had made straight for the bar. 'I thought he seemed very cheerful today. He had more colour in his cheeks, less of that grey pallor.' Uncorking a bottle of wine, he poured Harper a glass and handed it to her.

'Yes, that's true.'

She watched as Vieri dropped ice cubes into his glass, pouring in a generous measure of whisky. With his shirtsleeves rolled up, his hair casually messed, he was the epitome of the billionaire playboy at ease. He was strikingly tall, his physique a perfect combination of long limbs and honed muscle beneath taut olive skin, his movements both graceful and dangerous, like a tiger on the prowl. Yes, he was far more handsome than was good for him. Or her for that matter. Despite her best intentions to remain aloof, he seemed to have the bizarre capacity to heat her skin from within whenever he looked at her, to set her body tingling with anticipation at the mere sound of his faint, but deeply sexy Sicilian accent.

Taking a healthy sip of her wine, she turned away. She knew she had to be on her guard. She knew she really, really shouldn't be starting to look forward to this brief, early evening time they spent together. It wasn't as if Vieri had ever given her the slightest encouragement, shown any interest in her at all.

In the few days since arriving in Sicily they had fallen into a routine of sorts. Vieri would work all morning while Harper was left to amuse herself. She had taken to wandering into Palermo, exploring the narrow, cobbled side streets and the exotic markets or ordering a cup of bitter dark coffee and sitting outside to watch the bustling crowds go by. The city was full of such colour and vibrancy, she was already starting to love it. Their afternoons would be spent visiting Alfonso and then in the evening Vieri would disappear into his office and she wouldn't see him again. Despite being able to choose from the hotel's extensive menu, prepared by one of Sicily's top chefs, Harper had little appetite. Eating alone on the sofa, she would spend her time making calls to her father or searching social media sites on the Internet in the hope of finding some information about Leah. But there was nothing. Which only made her worry deepen still further.

Now she moved to sit on one of the cream leather sofas. 'I did think Alfonso was looking better today, but that doesn't alter the fact that he knows our engagement is a sham. You underestimate how sharp he is.'

'I can assure you I never underestimate anything about my godfather.' Vieri seated himself on the sofa opposite her, the ice clinking in the glass. He sounded vaguely irritated, as if she was a slightly annoying appendage that had to be tolerated in order to solve a problem. Which she supposed she was. But the more he treated her like that, the more Harper found she couldn't hold her tongue. She was forthright by nature, and if something needed to be said, she couldn't help but say it. Even if every broodingly dark muscle of Vieri's finely honed body was silently telling her to shut up.

'Then you must have noticed the way he looks at us, the way he takes everything in. He is not fooled by our pretence for a minute, Vieri. If you think he believes us, the only one being fooled is you.'

A muscle twitched ominously in Vieri's cheek, silently conveying just how close she had come to overstepping the mark.

'Well.' With an exhalation of breath he leant back into the sofa, crossing one long leg over the other, his relaxed posture not fooling Harper for a minute. 'As you seem to be so much more perceptive than me perhaps you would like to suggest what we do about it.'

'Fine, I will.' Refusing to be cowed, Harper placed her glass down on the table beside her. It was already half finished. She was drinking far too quickly. 'First off we need to look as if we like each other—that would be a good start. Make eye contact, for example.'

'I wasn't aware we didn't do that.'

'Really? You spend more time looking at Alfonso's nurse than you do me.'

Vieri gave a wry laugh. 'Not jealous are we, Harper?'

'Hardly.' Her reply was too fast, too vehement. 'Why would I be?'

'Why indeed?' Dark brows quirked upwards. 'So, lack of eye contact, duly noted. What else am I doing wrong? I'm sure you are bursting to tell me.'

Harper frowned as she scanned his supremely confident pose. Yes, there were several things that she would be only too happy to point out to him, but many more she would keep to herself. Like the frantic beat of her blood when she was faced with that midnight-blue stare of his. And the fact that, far from lessening on a longer acquaintance, the impact of his powerful persona and stunning good looks seemed to be having an even more potent effect on her nervous system.

He altered his position, uncrossing his legs and running a hand over his jaw. For all his arrogant ease, Harper could see that he was waiting to hear what she had to say, even if he did intend to totally disregard it. Because beneath that languid exterior, Vieri Romano was as stubborn and unyielding as an iron girder. Well, fine, she was stubborn too. Something her father liked to hurl at her, along with a lot more colourful adjectives, when he couldn't get her to procure another bottle of whisky for him from the bar at the Lodge, or give him the money so that he could stumble down to the pub for himself.

'Well, your body language is all wrong,' she

began purposefully. Vieri had asked for his short-comings so she would give them to him. It was too good an opportunity to miss. 'And you are far too evasive when Alfonso asks you questions about us. And you jump in all the time, when he is trying to talk to me.'

'Is that so? Clearly I am no good at this.' Vieri took another sip of whisky and set the glass down beside him. 'So, shifty-eyed, stilted posture, eva-sive and interfering. Is there anything else you would like to add?'

'No.' Harper pursed her lips to suppress a rogue smile. 'I think that's enough to be going on with.'

'*Bene*, then we had better do something about it.'

Harper's smile knotted inside her. Something about the glint in his eye told her she wasn't going to like what was coming next. Ditto, his use of the word *we*.

'What do you mean?'

'I suggest we try some role play.' Somehow he managed to make the idea burn with seduc-tive intent.

Harper's anxiety spiked. 'Role play?'

'Yes.' His eyes travelled lazily over her increas-ingly tense frame. 'A little role play will help us be more comfortable in one another's presence.'

Being in Vieri's presence made Harper feel

many things but *comfortable* wasn't one of them. And she strongly suspected that the sort of role play he was talking about would do nothing to help with that.

'I'm not sure that's such a good idea.' She turned her head away, flustered, desperately trying to escape from the trap that was of her own making.

'No?' Rising to his feet, Vieri moved to stand in front of her. 'Well, it has to be worth a try. Come on, up you get.'

Holding out his hands towards her, he gave them an impatient shake.

Harper swallowed, her mind struggling to come up with something to veto this crazy idea, the excitement tingling through her disobedient body already making this impossible.

Slowly she reached out towards him, preparing herself for the inevitable jolt of awareness that shot through her whenever their hands touched. And yep, there it was again, like a fizz of electricity running through her.

Pulled to her feet, she found herself standing mere inches from Vieri's towering form, trapped by his height and power and sheer magnetic pull. And when Vieri lightly took hold of her shoulders, drawing her towards him, her heart, which was already beating double time, threatened to leap out of her chest altogether, to make a bid for freedom to prevent any further assaults on its ability to function.

But worse was to come. With a shudder of pleasure, Harper felt his hands skim over her shoulders and down her back, where they settled possessively on either side of her waist, spanning the waistband of her jeans. She tried to move beneath his possessive grip but that only brought her into closer contact with him and as their bodies joined she became acutely aware of his honed shape; the muscles that rippled beneath his broad shoulders, the granite-hard chest pressed against her breasts, the long limbs, one leg slowly edging between her own, sending a thrill of awareness through her as she sensed his growing arousal. Harper let out a gasp.

'Hmm.' Vieri moved his hands to her back and, lowering his head, whispered in her ear. 'Interesting.' Sweeping aside her hair, he very gently pressed his lips below her earlobe, before lightly travelling down the sweep of her neck. *Oh, dear Lord.* Eyes tightly closed, Harper involuntarily angled her head to allow him more access.

'It seems we have found a connection.' He raised his head and Harper opened her eyes to meet his. 'Perhaps this won't be as hard as we thought.'

Or a whole lot harder. Fighting to catch her breath, she moved inside his hold, intent on finding some control. But Vieri hadn't finished with her yet.

'Maybe we should try a kiss.' He looked at her as if she were some sort of experiment. 'In the interest of authenticity, I mean.'

'I really don't think that will be necess—'

But before she could even gasp out the words his mouth was on hers, with the lightest of touches, just resting there as if to see what might happen next. Harper's breath stalled. No way could this be construed as a passionate kiss, not yet, but that didn't stop it from feeling intimate, sexual, heavy with promise. With a thrilling certainty she knew just where this kiss could go, what it could lead to. And as Vieri increased the pressure she found herself responding, feeling the thrum of excitement explode inside her head as her lips parted and his tongue found hers, sliding against it, around it, softly persuasive, hot, wet and druggingly sensual, tasting and teasing in a way that made her whole body shake with longing. Pulling away, she just caught the briefest hint of surprise in his eyes before he lowered his head again to continue his relentless assault. She had no sense of how long it was before, light-headed from lack of air and the sheer, potent sexuality of the kiss, she finally managed to push herself away from him and drag in a gulp of air.

She tried to hide the tremble of her body. Never

had she imagined a kiss could be anything like that, so intensely hot and wild and powerful, leaving her knees shaking and her ears ringing. It wasn't as if she had never been kissed before. She had dated a couple of the local lads back home in Glenruie and it had been pleasant enough. Though not sufficiently pleasant for her to want to take the relationships much further. But she most certainly had never been kissed like *that* before. Thoroughly, utterly and completely possessed by a man who knew exactly what he was doing.

But it was just role play. Harper smoothed down her blouse, touching her lips with shaking fingers to check they were still there, that they hadn't somehow melted or fused with the heat. What they had just done wasn't real—whatever else, she had to remember that. Except now, of course, he had totally ruined her for any other man's touch. Thanks for that, Mr Romano.

Bracing herself, she raised her eyes to meet his. And there it was, that assurance, the deeply held complacency of a man who knew exactly the effect he had had on her. It was almost as if he had branded her as his own. Well, they would see about that.

'That's quite enough of that.' She deliberately moved away from him.

'Really?' A wicked smile played around his

lips. 'I was just starting to enjoy myself. I believe you were too.'

'Whether or not either of us enjoyed it is entirely of no consequence.' Harper pulled at the neck of her blouse. Why was it so damned hot in here?

'Oh, I don't know. I found it of considerable consequence.' Mocking dark brows raised fractionally. 'You may have noticed.'

Harper flushed violently. Why was it that Vieri was crowing over his physical attraction to her, whereas she felt she had to frantically try and cover it up? Because Vieri had been in control, that was why. Because he was used to seducing women, no doubt bedding a different woman every night, revelling in the power he had over them, using them to satisfy his casual sexual urges and then discarding them without a second thought. It was written all over his smugly arrogant face.

Well, there was no way she was going to fall for his smooth, well-practised seduction routine, no matter how good it might have felt.

'We were supposed to be learning how to be easy around one another in front of Alfonso to try and make our engagement believable. Not getting involved with…' she hesitated, hating the breathless catch in her voice, the way her cheeks still burned '…that sort of thing.'

'That sort of thing?' He was deliberately mocking her, loving every moment of her discomfort.

'Yes.' Her voice went up a notch. 'You know perfectly well what I'm talking about.'

He certainly did. Vieri let his eyes travel slowly over her flushed face, lingering on the swollen pout of her mouth. His very physical reaction to her had taken him by surprise, as clearly it had her, the passionate nature of the kiss catching him unawares. He had thought himself firmly in control, never doubted it for a second but somehow, lost in the heat of Harper's mouth, that control had slipped dangerously. In fact, if Harper hadn't called time on their little role-playing exercise he wasn't sure he would have had the willpower to do so himself. And then where would they be? In bed, that was where, at least if he'd had any say in the matter.

The image of Harper splayed across his bed had lodged in his mind and refused to be shifted. Her copper-coloured hair spread across the pillows, that shapely figure of hers waiting to be divested of its clothes, the no doubt sensible underwear he'd find and the pleasure he would take in slowly removing it. There was something incredibly sexy about Harper McDonald, something he couldn't quite put his finger on, though his traitorous body would have him putting his finger pretty much everywhere. And that would be just the start.

He gazed at her now, at the way those remarkable tawny eyes glittered with a mixture of arousal and defiance. She really had no idea how attractive she was and that made a welcome change from the sort of women he usually found himself surrounded with who, frankly, suffered from the opposite problem. But it was more than that. There was an earthiness to her, a sensuality that was entirely unwitting, just a part of who she was. Perhaps it was her Scottish heritage. Somehow she conjured up purple heather and damp bracken and soft green moss and how it would feel to lay her down on such a bed and make love to her.

Enough! Moving a couple of steps away, he adjusted the fit of his trousers. Taking Harper to bed was not part of the plan. He just needed to remember that.

'Well—' he adopted a businesslike approach '—if you are sure we are done here, I will go and get on with some work.'

Turning to leave, he had reached the doorway when he remembered something. 'Oh, by the way.' He looked back to where Harper was still rooted to the spot. 'I meant to say, there is a charity gala here in Palermo on Saturday. Alfonso is a patron. He would like us to go.'

'Oh, right.' She didn't even try to hide the despondency in her voice and for some reason that riled him. He wasn't used to his dates being anything less than wildly enthusiastic when they were chosen to accompany him to glittering social events.

'You will need an appropriate outfit.' He raked his eyes dismissively over her casual jeans-and-top ensemble. 'In fact, you should choose several outfits. There may be a number of social engagements we need to attend while we are here.'

'I see.'

'My driver will be at your disposal. And obviously you will charge everything to my account.' Still she refused to look remotely grateful. Weren't women supposed to like shopping? 'I trust that won't be a problem?'

'No problem at all.' She tipped her chin haughtily. 'It's your money.'

'Indeed it is. And you are, to all intents and purposes, my fiancée.' Mounting irritation scored his voice. 'So please make sure you choose appropriately.'

'Yes, sir.' She tossed her hair dramatically over her shoulder. 'Heaven forbid that I should embarrass you in any way.'

Vieri ground down on his jaw. Embarrassment was not one of the emotions this infuriating young woman stirred up in him. But right now he had no intention of examining the ones that she did.

'*Bene*, that's settled, then.' He turned and strode from the room. Suddenly the need to put some space between them seemed vitally important.

CHAPTER FOUR

HARPER HAD TO admit that there was a certain heady excitement about going into these exclusive designer boutiques and knowing she could buy anything she wanted. At the mention of Vieri Romano's name, the snooty shop assistants were falling over themselves to help her, parading a dazzling array of garments before her. In the end she bought a cocktail dress, a pair of tailored trousers and a fitted jacket, all of which, she decided sourly, would be considered sufficiently appropriate.

But still no ball gown. As she breathed in the expensively scented air of yet another boutique, Harper determined that she would not leave this one without the requisite purchase. She was quite sure that there were any number of beautiful dresses here that would be more than suitable. The fact that she didn't feel right in any of them was because of the circumstances, not the gowns.

Finally she made her choice, a dark green lightweight velvet creation with a demure neckline and a full-length skirt. It was considerably less daring than some of the outfits, which was why she picked it. She didn't want to feel sexy around Vieri. Not when just the memory of that clinch, that kiss, was enough to set her knees wobbling again.

She was arranging to have it delivered to the hotel when she was interrupted by a tall, striking-looking middle-aged woman who she had noticed idly flicking through a rail of clothes and who had now silently come to stand beside her.

'Excuse me.'

Harper turned and gave her a friendly smile. It wasn't returned.

'Did I hear you say that you are a guest of Vieri Romano?' The woman spoke perfect English.

'Yes.' Harper wasn't sure what business it was of hers but she politely replied.

'How very interesting.' Perfectly made-up eyes swept over her from top to toe, taking in every little detail until Harper felt she was staring at her very bones. 'And that outfit you are buying.' She pointed a manicured finger at the dress being held by the sales assistant. 'It is for the Winter Ball?'

'Yes, that's right.'

'Then how fortunate for you that we bumped

into each other. A dress like that will never do. Vieri will hate it.'

Harper frowned. She didn't like being spoken to like this by a woman she didn't know from Adam. In fact, instinctively she didn't like this woman at all, but, positioned firmly beside her as she was, she was impossible to ignore. Sensing Harper's reluctance, the woman gave her a forced smile.

'How rude you must think me, my dear.' She extended a hand weighed down with jewelled rings. 'Allow me to introduce myself. My name is Donatella Sorrentino. I am an old friend of Vieri's.'

'Harper McDonald.' Harper took her hand but found herself pulled into an awkward embrace, the soft fur of the woman's mink coat crushed against her chest as several heavily perfumed air kisses were wafted on either side of her. Pulling away, Donatella studied her with highly critical eyes.

'So tell me, Harper McDonald, how do you come to be accompanying Vieri to the ball?'

Harper moved a step away. 'Alfonso, Vieri's godfather, is a patron of the charity that hosts the ball.'

'You hardly need to tell me that, my dear.' Donatella's eyes glittered coldly. 'I suspect I know rather more about Sicilian society than you do.

And quite apart from that, Alfonso Calleroni is my uncle.'

'Oh.' Harper was suitably chastened. 'I'm sorry, I didn't know.'

'Why would you? How is the old man, by the way?' She only just managed to stifle a bored yawn. 'I have been meaning to pay him a visit.'

'He is very frail.' Harper chose her words carefully. She wasn't going to be the one to tell this woman her uncle was dying, even if she suspected she wouldn't give a damn. 'But I think having Vieri here is cheering him up.'

'I'm sure. And you? Where do you fit into this cosy little scenario?'

Harper hesitated. Apart from Alfonso, no one else knew about their engagement and she only ever wore the tell-tale ring when they were visiting him. To tell a woman like this, who looked as if *malicious gossip* could be her middle names, might be a dangerous thing. But on the other hand, what did it matter? People were bound to find out sooner or later and frankly the temptation to try and shock that supercilious face out of its Botoxed grimace was too great to resist. She took in a breath.

'I am Vieri's fiancée.'

The look of total astonishment on Donatella's face was so great that Harper wasn't sure she had actually taken the information in. She decided to clarify, just for good measure. 'We are engaged to be married.'

'Mio Dio!' The words rasped from her throat before Donatella had time to stop them. But she quickly recovered herself. 'How simply wonderful. Come, let me embrace you.' She tugged Harper against her again, speaking over her shoulder. 'Why, that means we are almost family.'

Harper suppressed a shudder. If she had thought her own family was bad enough, this woman was on another level altogether.

Pulling away, Donatella held her at arm's length, gripping her shoulders that bit too hard with bony hands that felt more like claws. 'To think that Vieri is finally to marry. You must tell me simply everything, my dear, where you met, how you came to fall in love, although Vieri of course has always been totally irresistible and you...you are such a pretty young thing. When is the wedding to be? This is all so romantic!' She was babbling now, the words coming out in a rabid torrent. 'We must have lunch.' Fishing in her bag, she produced a diary, hurriedly flicking through the pages. 'Now, let me see—'

'That's very kind of you,' Harper interrupted, 'but I can't give you a date right now. I'm not really sure what my plans are.'

This brought Donatella's head back up. '*Your* plans?' Immediately she pounced on Harper's mistake. 'I'm sure Vieri will have everything mapped out for you both. He has always been so frightfully organised. When did you say the wedding was?'

'I didn't,' Harper replied firmly. 'We haven't fixed a date yet.'

'So this is all quite sudden?' Cold blue eyes drilled into her. 'You haven't known Vieri very long?'

'Not long, no.'

'I thought as much. You would never be considering buying that ghastly dress if you knew Vieri like I do. Look…' she glanced at her watch '… I can give you fifteen minutes. At least let me choose a suitable dress for you.' She moved over to the rails, snapping her fingers at the sales assistants, who rushed to her side to take hold of the garments she was rapidly selecting in a frantic rustle of taffeta and silk.

'Now run along and try these on and I will wait here to give you my final verdict.' She decorously draped herself on a velvet chaise longue, all eagle-eyed determination.

'We can't have you letting our Vieri down, now, can we?'

Sitting at the pavement café, Vieri took a sip of his espresso and opened his newspaper. His morning had gone well, a successful business meeting seeing him acquire a large plot of land ripe for development to add to his portfolio here in Sicily. And right now, even though he had vowed never to live here again, he couldn't deny that being back in Palermo felt good, felt like coming home.

A flash of auburn-coloured hair across the road caught his eye and suddenly there was Harper, striding along in the sunshine, her shoulder bag bouncing against her side. She seemed completely oblivious to the admiring glances of the men around her but Vieri wasn't. He found his grip tightening on the handle of his cup.

In truth, seeing her here wasn't entirely coincidental. At breakfast that morning she had told him she was going to visit the antiquities museum, which happened to be just around the corner. He had offered her a lift into town with him, which of course she had declined. It seemed she preferred to walk.

Now he watched as she bent down to stroke the head of a mangy-looking dog belonging to a beggar sheltering in a doorway. Vieri closed his newspaper, observing them intently. He saw Harper take her purse from her bag, pull out some notes, then turn the purse to shake out the coins before offering the whole lot to the man, who was getting to his feet, his hands cupped before him eagerly. Vieri stood up, his protective instinct on high alert. The beggar was pulling Harper towards him, either in some sort of embrace, or he was about to go through her pockets—or worse. Whichever, it was enough to see Vieri leap through two lanes of traffic with horns blaring, to land by her side.

'That's enough.' Speaking in Sicilian he pulled the man away by his shoulder, the beggar looking at him with a mixture of annoyance and surprise. 'Get your hands off her.'

'Vieri!' Harper rounded on him in outrage. 'What do you think you're doing?'

'I could ask the same of you.' Moving his hand to the small of her back, he propelled her forward along the pavement, tucking her arm through his to secure her to his side. 'I just saw you giving him the entire contents of your purse.'

'So what if I did.' She tripped angrily along beside him. 'It wasn't your money, if that's what you're worried about.'

'I don't give a damn about the money.' He navigated them between the pedestrians. 'But I do worry about you getting yourself into dangerous situations.'

'Well, don't. I can take care of myself. And besides, there was nothing dangerous about that. The poor man was hungry, that's all, and so was the dog.'

'That's as may be. But that doesn't mean he's not a violent criminal.'

'Oh, for God's sake!' Jerking to a halt, Harper pulled her arm from under his and held it across her chest. 'I don't know how you live like that, thinking the worst of everyone. I feel sorry for you, I really do.'

'Save your pity for the beggars, *cara*.' He met her heated stare full on. 'And besides, I don't think the worst of everyone. When it came to your sister it seems I didn't think badly enough.'

He watched, not without some satisfaction, as the famous pout put in another appearance. She really had the most luscious lips, pink and full and perfectly formed. It was all he could do to stop himself from raising his fingers to touch them or, better still, bending his head to feel them against his own. The fact was, he hadn't been the same since that kiss they had shared. Even though a couple of days had passed, the memory of it still burned in his head—in his groin.

At the time he had pretended he was doing it to test Harper, to see how she would react. With arousal already stirring in his body he had wanted confirmation that she was feeling it too—at least that was what he'd told himself. But the fact was, the sight of those swollen lips had been impossible to resist, especially when coupled with her heavy-lidded eyes and that sensuous take-me-to-bed body.

That, at least, he had managed to force himself to resist. So far anyway. Harper's bedroom was at the opposite end of the hotel apartment from his and he had expressly forbidden himself from going anywhere near it. Just the thought of the delights that lay in wait for him on the other side of that door was enough to see him heading for the shower and swinging the dial round to cold.

If anyone had told him that he would be obsessing over this relatively ordinary young Scottish woman he would have told them they were mad. She was not his type, she wasn't glamorous or sophisticated or worldly. But she was warm and clever and kind. Despite the telling-off he had given her, the compassion she had shown that beggar, the way she had let him pull her into his arms, even though he must have smelled decidedly rank, had touched Vieri. It was typical of her, always thinking of others. Couple that with a natural prettiness and an innate sexiness and you had a special kind of person. Had he just called her *ordinary*? Who was he trying to kid?

But she was also as stubborn as a mule. Linking his arm through hers once more, he started them walking again. His car was parked only a few streets away. He wasn't even going to tell her that he'd just decided he was taking her out for lunch. She'd only start kicking up a fuss.

'So.' He turned them down a side street. 'Did you enjoy the antiquities museum?'

'Yes, I did.' He felt her relief at the change of subject. 'There are some amazing works of art in there. It's hard to believe that some of them date back thousands of years.'

'Sicily has a very rich history.'

'But some things never change.' Following her gaze, he saw she had spotted another beggar on the other side of the street. He groaned inwardly, preparing himself for another lecture. And sure enough it soon came. 'Doesn't it bother you?' She shot him an upward glance. 'Living a life of such wealth and privilege, when there is still so much poverty all around?'

Vieri drew in an exasperated breath. 'For your information, I have earned the life that I lead through hard work and determination.' He had no idea why he felt the need to defend himself, why he should give a toss what this opinionated young woman thought of him. He only knew that he did. 'And quite apart from that, me living like a pauper is not going to help these guys.' He gestured across the road. 'But by continuing to invest in this country I am providing employment and security for families who in turn pay taxes that go towards helping those less fortunate. Plus

I am actively involved with a number of charities. Throwing down a handful of coins is not the long-term solution.'

'Well, no, I suppose not,' she conceded quietly. 'But sometimes a short-term solution is better than nothing.' Their eyes clashed before Harper dragged her gaze away. 'Oh…' She looked around her, suddenly realising they had stopped. 'Is this your car?'

'It is.' Opening the door, Vieri gestured to her to get inside. 'If you would like to get in, I know a nice restaurant not far along the coast. I thought I could buy you lunch before we go and see Alfonso this afternoon. That is, if your socialist principles will allow it, of course.'

Harper hesitated, biting down on her lip. Unless Vieri was very much mistaken she was trying to hide the hint of a smile. Finally she slipped into the passenger seat and turned to face him as he got in beside her, tucking her hair behind her ears. And there it was, the distinct and heart-warming twinkle of mirth dancing in those autumn-coloured eyes.

'Lunch would be lovely.' She even reached out to touch his arm, albeit very briefly. 'Thank you.'

Through the arched windows of the overheated sitting room, Vieri watched Harper and his god-father in the garden. Bundled up in a thick coat and with a rug across his knees, Alfonso was seated in his wheelchair, Harper slowly pushing him along the neat paths that meandered between flower beds that had more bare earth than flowers at this time of year.

Alfonso had been quite determined that he wanted to go out and get some fresh air, and that it should be Harper, and Harper alone, who was to accompany him. His nurse, Maria, had been told to take some time for herself and Vieri, somewhat unwillingly, left to his own devices.

They had stopped now, Harper coming round to Alfonso's side, squatting down so that she was level with him. Alfonso was pointing to a bird perched on a holly bush, a goldfinch if Vieri wasn't mistaken, though he was no expert on ornithology. He was more interested in the way Harper's hand rested on Alfonso's knee, the way Alfonso's own hand went to protectively cover it. The bird flew off and Harper tucked in the scarf around Alfonso's neck and they smiled at each other before she stood up and went back to pushing the wheelchair.

Vieri frowned. His godfather clearly adored Harper. And she him, if the tender way she fussed over him was anything to go by. Vieri had noticed the way Maria had started to defer to her, obviously happy that Alfonso was in safe hands when Harper was around.

Turning away, he sat himself down on the ancient sofa, drumming his fingers on the cracked leather of the arm as he waited for them to return. It was good that they got on so well, that Alfonso so obviously approved of his choice of 'fiancée'. But at the same time, it left him with more than a slight sense of unease. Somehow this close friendship they were forming troubled him because of course it was all built on a lie. Somehow it would have been easier if they had remained more emotionally distant from one another, then Vieri wouldn't have ended up feeling such a fraud. He was starting to realise that he hadn't thought this thing through at all.

His lunch with Harper had been surprisingly relaxed. Choosing the fresh catch of the day, Harper had ploughed her way through a large platter of seafood with surprising speed, enthusiastically mopping up the juices with hunks of bread. It had been a real delight to see her enjoying her food, although Vieri had been careful to avert his eyes to the twinkling expanse of the Mediterranean Sea when she had finally come up for air, dabbing her mouth with the napkin and declaring it was the nicest meal she had ever had. Even so, he felt a foolish swell of pride that he had finally managed to do something that had made her happy.

A buzz from his phone alerted him to a new

email message from Bernie, his head of security. Vieri clicked it open. Rodriguez had been found and was back in New York. But Leah McDonald was no longer with him. Bernie was awaiting further instructions. Vieri narrowed his eyes for a moment, then tapped out his reply.

Leave Rodriguez to me. Find Leah McDonald asap.

He heard a door opening and the sound of Harper and his godfather returning. Harper was laughing at something Alfonso had said and when they appeared in the sitting room she was still smiling, her cheeks flushed from the cold, her hair a mass of untamed curls. She looked…gorgeous. Dragging his gaze away, he was suddenly conscious of Alfonso's eyes on him, a knowing smile playing about his lips.

'Let me help you into your chair, *padrino*.' For some unknown reason he felt flustered, as if he had been exposed. 'I do hope you haven't caught a chill.'

'Stop fussing, my boy, I am fine. With your fiancée, I have been in the very best hands.' He smiled at Harper before easing himself into his chair. 'But I think I will go for a lie-down in a minute. Harper, perhaps you would be so good as to find Maria for me.'

'Of course.'

As she left the room, Alfonso signalled to Vieri to close the door behind her.

'Come here, my son. Quickly. I want to talk to you before Harper returns.'

Vieri pulled up a wooden chair and seated himself opposite his godfather.

'What is it, *padrino*?'

'I may be old,' he started, fixing his godson with a watery stare, 'but I like to think I am still pretty astute.'

'Indeed you are.' Vieri didn't doubt that for a second.

'And it is fairly obvious to me that you have rushed ahead with this engagement because you want to make your old godfather happy.'

Vieri inhaled sharply. Was this it? Had they been rumbled? Had Harper been right all along? With Alfonso's penetrating gaze firmly trained on his face, Vieri decided that if necessary he would come clean, admit that this was all a sham. He wasn't prepared to dig the hole of this lie any deeper.

'And I want you to know that you have succeeded.' His lined face lit up. 'Harper is a wonderful girl. I am delighted that you have fallen in love with someone so perfect for you.' He raised his eyebrows.

'Well...yes, thank you,' Vieri mumbled quietly.

'In fact I would go as far as to say you are

very lucky to have found her. Young women like Harper are few and far between. Don't lose her, Vieri.'

'I'll try not to.'

But his attempt to be light-hearted was met with a sudden seriousness as Alfonso reached to take hold of his hand.

'I mean it.' His eyes glittered. 'You have to trust me on this one. As someone who probably knows you better than you know yourself, I'm telling you, if you let Harper slip through your fingers you will regret it.'

'Alfonso—'

'No, hear me out, *figlio*. As you know, I never married, never had a family, not because I didn't want to but because of the terrible vendetta between my family and the Sorrentinos. The vendetta that took the life of my dear brother.' Alfonso's voice faltered but with a look of grim determination he carried on. 'Now I am the very last Calleroni so when I die the name will die with me and the generations of murder can finally cease.'

'I know this, *padrino*.' Vieri's voice was soft. 'I have always known.'

'And you also know that this is the reason that I could never adopt you as my son, much as I wanted to, because I would never burden you with the Calleroni name.'

'I do, *padrino*. But to be your godson has been more than honour enough.'

'And it has been my pleasure. To see the success you have made of your life has been my greatest achievement. Especially...' He paused and reached for a glass of water by his side to moisten his throat. 'Especially as there were times, in the early days, when I thought I had lost you.'

'Never, *padrino*. I would never have turned my back on you.'

But they both knew the time that Alfonso referred to. That black period in Vieri's youth when the course of his life could so easily have changed for ever. Or more likely ended—with a bullet through his head.

Vieri had been just eighteen, little more than a kid, when Donatella Sorrentino had deliberately sought out her uncle's handsome young protégé. At the time she had appeared to Vieri to be the height of sophistication: wealthy, extremely attractive and impossibly glamorous. He had known she was dangerous, but in Vieri's naive eyes that had only made her all the more alluring.

Some years before, Donatella Calleroni, as she had been then, had done the unthinkable and crossed the divide, forsaking her own family to marry into the Sorrentino dynasty. The fallout between the two warring clans had been predictably catastrophic. In the name of honour but blinded by revenge, her father, Eduardo Calleroni, had retaliated in the only way he knew how—with violence, ending up with him splattered across the tarmac in a hail of bullets. His brother's death had broken Alfonso's heart but if Donatella had felt any guilt, any remorse, she never had shown it.

But even knowing all this, to Vieri's intense shame, he had still fallen under her spell.

In hindsight he could see how he had been groomed. Donatella had taken such an interest in him, buying him clothes, taking him to the theatre, the opera, for meals out in expensive restaurants. By keeping her entertained Vieri was doing her husband a favour, she had insisted, because Frank never did anything but work.

In actual fact Frank Sorrentino had known full well what was going on, to start with at least. One of Sicily's most notorious gangsters, he had thought it wise to keep tabs on the clever Romano boy who was a son in all but name to Alfonso Calleroni. Donatella had been dispatched to keep a close eye on him. Something she had done all too well.

Before long the idea of them going to bed together had shifted from an erotic fantasy to an inevitability. And Vieri, still a virgin, had wanted it, badly. The thought of Donatella being his first, maybe even his only, had filled his head, consumed his young body, sent his teenage hormones into overdrive. So he had readily agreed to Donatella's terms that nobody could ever, *ever* discover their illicit relationship. Despite knowing the possible consequences, they had embarked on a passionate affair.

And then, as suddenly as it had begun, it was over. Donatella was bored, she told him. He was becoming too possessive, anyway he was far too young for her. It was only ever meant to have been a brief fling. From being a constant presence in his life she abruptly severed all contact.

And Vieri had accepted her decision, respected her wishes. Despite being shocked, bruised, broken-hearted even, for he had genuinely believed himself to be in love with her, he had backed right off, walked away. Done as he was told.

It was only several months later that he had discovered the full, horrifying truth. And such had been his all-consuming rage, his thirst for revenge, that he knew he would have been capable of almost anything. With fire raging in his blood and his contacts in the world of organised crime, the situation could so easily have ended in disaster, destruction, death.

But then Alfonso had stepped in. Without ever discussing anything a position in New York had rapidly been found for him, together with a considerable amount of money to enable him to make a new life for himself. Which of course he had done, becoming a billionaire businessman in under ten years. He had his godfather to thank for his success. But more than that, he had him to thank for his life.

Now he squeezed Alfonso's hand. 'You know you mean the world to me, *padrino*.'

'I do indeed, *mio figlio*. Which is why you are going to accept this one piece of advice.' His voice quavered. 'Build a family for yourself, Vieri, a wife and children. Don't live an empty life like mine.'

'You have not led an empty life, Alfonso! How can you even say that?'

'It has been empty in here.' He punched at his bony chest with a frail fist. 'Inside, where it matters. I had to deliberately end my family line but you, you have the chance to start one. Don't you see, Vieri, by being an orphan, by having no background, you have a blank canvas? You are free from the shackles that restrained me. Make the most of that opportunity.'

'What are you saying?'

'I'm saying it is time to alter the course of your life. Don't put it off any longer. Take this opportunity to marry your lovely fiancée and settle down.'

'Alfonso, I—'

'Set a date, Vieri.'

'I'm sorry?'

'For the wedding, set a date. And don't make it too far away. If I am to stand any chance of seeing you two walk down the aisle it will need to be within the next month.'

CHAPTER FIVE

HARPER SURVEYED HERSELF in the full-length mirror. She had to admit that awful Sorrentino woman had chosen the most beautiful dress, even though she would never have picked it for herself. Not in a thousand years.

Made of shimmering satin, it had a slim-fitting bodice, ingeniously styled so that the two straps only went over one shoulder leaving a tantalising sliver of cleavage in between and a wide expanse of bare back behind. Slightly ruched around the hips and bottom, it hugged her tightly, giving her a sexy shape she hadn't even known she had, before it fell in soft folds to the floor. But it was the colour that was the most shocking of all. Red. Bright red. Harper was quite sure that someone of her colouring should never wear red and yet here she was wearing it, and looking pretty darned hot—even if she did say so herself.

She turned, twisting to get a better view of the back, so intent on her own reflection that she failed to notice Vieri standing in the doorway of her dressing room.

'Molto bella.' His deep, sultry voice spun her around and she reached out a hand to steady herself against the dresser. As he slowly advanced towards her, her grip tightened against the polished wood. 'You have made a good choice.'

'Thank you.' His unexpected compliment went to her head like a glass of champagne. She was just about to blurt out that she hadn't actually chosen it herself but remembered Donatella's strict instructions that she wasn't to mention her input, or indeed that she had met her at all. Harper had wondered if it was because she had no intention of going to visit Alfonso, that maybe this was just a flying visit. Harper gathered she now lived in Milan. 'You look pretty smart yourself.'

Smart was a massive understatement. He looked completely, heart-stoppingly, drop-dead gorgeous. Wearing a tuxedo and a white dress shirt with a black bow tie, he was the epitome of suave, elegant handsomeness, as if he had been created solely for the purpose of showing how it should be done. Long limbs were effortlessly encased in the fine fabric, giving him an easy, cat-like grace. He was clean shaven, Harper noticed, his usual designer stubble missing, and his hair was still wet from the shower, pushed back from his forehead so that the thick dark curls were temporarily tamed. He smelled divine too, his subtle aftershave invading her senses now that he was so close. Too close. Way too close.

'Are you wearing your hair down?' Harper's breath stuttered to a halt as he reached forward to move her hair to one side, exposing the sweep of her neck. 'I think the dress would suit an up-style, don't you, maybe with some suitable earrings to set it off?'

'Maybe.' Harper pursed her lips. 'But I don't happen to have any suitable earrings.' What did he think, that she had a selection of diamond jewellery that she could dip into for any occasion?

'I wish I'd thought of that before.' Vieri's intense dark blue gaze seared into her. 'I would have bought you some.'

'Well, it doesn't matter.' With a small shake of her head, Harper dislodged his hand so that she could start to breathe again. By taking her caustic comment and turning it around with his offer to buy her jewellery he had disarmed her. More than that, something about the intensity of his stare was doing alarming things to her insides. She wasn't used to being the focus of such close attention, to have someone looking at her, really looking at her, almost as if they cared. She quickly brushed the silly notion away. 'I'll put my hair up anyway.'

Briskly sweeping past him, she fled for the

sanctuary of her bedroom where her make-up bag held a few grips and an assortment of hair bands. 'Do you want to wait for me down in the lobby?'

'That's okay. I'm fine here.'

Harper's heart plummeted. He might be *fine* there, decorously lounging about in her dressing room, but she felt anything but fine, as a quick glimpse in the mirror brutally revealed.

She looked different somehow, as if some sort of banned substance had entered her bloodstream, changing her features. It took her a second to work out what the peculiar look was, and when she did she wished she hadn't. Because it was arousal. Her cheeks were lightly flushed and her hazel eyes had darkened to a sultry amber glow as the devastating effect of his lethal attraction continued to pump in her veins.

This evening was going to be awful. However was she going to be able to stand beside Vieri, trying to be the elegant and sophisticated fiancée, when the merest touch of his breath on her neck did *this* to her?

Staring at the emerald ring on her finger, she fought the temptation to pull the wretched thing off and hurl it across the room. What good would that do? She had signed up to this deal—she had to see it through.

Picking up her hairbrush, she started to tug

it forcefully through her curls, giving herself a stern talking-to with each vicious stroke. Then, capturing the thick swathe of hair, she twisted it into a knot on the top of her head and, with a mouth full of hair grips, set about securing the stray tendrils as best she could. Then, setting her features in what she hoped was a suitably bland expression, she went back through to the dressing room.

Vieri, who had been sprawled in a chair, one long leg casually draped over the arm, rose to meet her. His blue eyes raked all over her but he made no comment as she brushed past him to retrieve the shoe box from the dresser, self-consciously lifting out the silver shoes and quickly slipping them onto her feet as if there were nothing remotely unusual about her wearing a pair of sparkly stilettos with a price tag that had made her eyes water, in much the same way as she suspected the shoes themselves would by the end of the night. Throwing a cashmere wrap around her shoulders, she then picked up the silver clutch bag and, drawing in a breath, turned to face Vieri again.

He came towards her, his right arm crooked as he waited for her to slide her arm through it. Nestled so closely beside him, Harper felt her pulse set off at a gallop.

'*Sei pronto*, you are ready?'

Harper nodded, although she felt anything but. She gathered the wrap closer to her in a vain attempt to ward off his nearness.

'Then let's go.'

As they moved towards the doorway Harper felt the wobble in her step. And it wasn't just the four-inch heels.

The Winter Ball was a magnificently glittering affair held in a stunning, floodlit medieval castle not far from Palermo. The guests were escorted across the moat and through the echoing anterooms to a ballroom that had been transformed into a winter wonderland. Giant icicles twirled above their heads, snowflakes danced across the walls, and enormous ice sculptures of fantastical beasts adorned the walls. It was certainly breathtaking, if a little dazzling. As Harper gazed about in awe she realised that most of the women were dressed in appropriately winter colours; ice blue was very popular, as were silver and white. Even the staff were dressed from head to toe in snowy white. And there she was in flaming scarlet.

'Why didn't you tell me?' she snapped in Vieri's ear as she reluctantly relinquished her wrap, the idea that she might be able to keep it on for the entire evening quickly taken out of her hands by the helpful cloakroom attendant.

'Tell you what?'

'That everyone would be dressed in…in cold colours.'

'I didn't know they would.' Vieri surveyed the room dismissively.

Harper followed his even gaze, feeling like a hedgerow poppy about to infiltrate a room full of lilies. But it was too late now. With his arm snaking around her waist, Vieri was confidently escorting her into the room, all eyes turning to look at them. Or so it seemed to Harper. She felt their curious stares, their blatant scrutiny of this boldly dressed stranger who had the audacity to be on the arm of Sicily's most eligible bachelor. As they advanced further into the room the crowd parted, almost reverentially, to let them through until a middle-aged man came forward to shake Vieri's hand, demanding to know who this beautiful young woman was. When Vieri casually introduced her as his fiancée there was an audible intake of breath before a group of people closed around them, congratulations flying as the women edged forward to get a better look at her, eyeing the ring on her finger with burning curiosity, while the men were slapping Vieri on the back.

Harper quickly downed half a glass of champagne. She was about as far out of her comfort zone as it was possible to go. Unlike her sister, she had never aspired to live the high life, the affairs of the rich and famous holding no interest for her. While Leah would be poring over celebrity magazines, she would be more likely to be found running her finger down the column of barely legible figures in their father's accounts ledger, trying to make sure that everything balanced before it was handed over to the estate accountant. Her biggest dread was that the Laird would be forced to sack her father, that they would lose their livelihood, their home. Gordon Gillespie, Laird of Craigmore, was a good man but fundamentally the Craigmore estate was a business, and if Angus McDonald was seen as a liability, Harper knew he would have to go. Which was why she worried herself sick fighting the losing battle to keep him sober, covering his tracks, essentially doing as much of his job as she could for him.

But tonight she had another job to do. Tonight she had to play the part of the adoring fiancée. Although how she was supposed to do that when Vieri was virtually ignoring her, she had no idea. Despite the fact that he had stressed in the car the importance of them giving a convincing performance because the gossip from the night would be sure to find its way back to Alfonso, now they were actually here he seemed to have forgotten all about her. As the great and the good of Sicilian high society swarmed around them, not to mention royalty and A-list celebrities from all over Europe, she watched him being borne away on a tide of adoring females, scarcely giving her a glance as he disappeared into the crowd. Well, maybe it was a much-needed reality check. When Vieri had looked at her in her dressing room, just for that moment, he had made her feel beautiful. He had made her feel *special*. Now, as she watched the smooth way he charmed the women around him, she realised it had simply been an act. A minor charm offensive. And like a fool she had fallen for it.

Draining the last of the champagne, she swapped the empty glass for a full one from a passing waiter. She wished she could shrink into the background, pretend she wasn't here, but, given her choice of attire, that wouldn't be easy. A shriek of laughter turned her head in time to see a beautiful blonde with icicle earrings grasp Vieri's arm then lean forward to giggle something into his ear. Harper turned back, squashing down the pang of hurt, refusing to let herself feel anything.

'*Signorina?*' A rather dashing young man wearing some sort of military uniform stepped forward. 'Would you do me the great honour of having the next dance?'

Pasting on a smile and accepting his hand, Harper allowed herself to be led to the dance floor, grateful that at least someone was paying her some attention. She would allow him the honour, and anyone else who might want to dance with her. They would be no substitute for Vieri, of course, but right now her bruised confidence would take anything that was on offer.

From his table at the side of the ballroom, Vieri's narrow-eyed gaze flitted across the crowded dance floor. She wasn't difficult to spot, the flash of that scarlet dress as Harper was twirled around by yet another partner, male guests of all ages queuing up for the chance to take her hand, slide their arm around her waist, hold her just that little bit too close.

Well, it was time to put a stop to it. Vieri pushed his drink away and rose to his feet. He thought he had made himself clear. He thought he had explained that her role as his 'fiancée' was to spend the evening by his side, look decorous and say little. Instead of that she had disappeared the first chance she'd had, already on the dance floor when he had looked up to see where she was within minutes of their arrival.

Irritation spiked through him, along with some other emotion that felt suspiciously like jealousy. He ground his jaw. If she was dancing with anyone it should be him.

Was she doing this deliberately? Trying to

prove some sort of point? Vieri had never concerned himself with the inner workings of a woman's mind and he certainly had no time for playing silly games, as the few women who had tried that on with him had soon found out to their cost. But he would never have thought that of Harper. She was too open, altogether too straightforward. It was one of the things he liked about her. But tonight she had overstepped the mark. If she wasn't playing games it was time he reminded her of her duty. To him.

Weaving his way through the dancers, he zoned in on his target, briefly pausing behind the swaying figure of Harper's partner, Hans Langenberg, the Crown Prince of a small European principality, before tapping him briskly on the shoulder.

'Excuse me.'

'Vieri Romano.' Hans turned to face him. 'I hope you haven't come to spoil my fun.'

'If you mean claiming my fiancée for a dance, then yes, I have.'

'Fiancée, eh, Romano?' The Crown Prince looked at him with renewed respect. 'So it's true. You are finally committing after all this time?'

Vieri gave a brisk nod. 'I said so, didn't I?'

'Well, hats off to you, old chap. You have made an excellent choice.'

Vieri scowled. Why did everyone persist in telling him what an excellent choice he had made when in point of fact he hadn't made the choice at all?

'Though I can't pretend I'm not disappointed,' Hans continued. 'I was hoping I might be in with a chance myself.'

'Well, I can assure you, you are not.' With a surge of possessiveness Vieri stepped in between the two of them, slipping his arm around Harper's waist. A tingle of awareness shot through him as his fingers touched the bare skin of her lower back. Swiftly followed by the hot rush of annoyance when he thought of the other men who had had their hands there tonight.

'I am here, you know, I can speak for myself,' Harper finally piped up. But her voice held none of the usual edge Vieri had expected to hear. Instead there was a hint of triumph, a light in her eyes that told him he had been sussed—that he had given himself away. Something she decided to put to the test by leaning into him so that the sexy warmth of her body worked its way through the fabric of his suit, setting off a chain reaction that he battled to contain.

'I don't doubt it for one moment, Miss McDonald.' Hans reached for Harper's hand, kissing the back of it before letting go and giving her a formal bow. 'Can I just say it has been a pleasure? And should you, you know, ever change your mind…'

There was a low growl and it took Vieri a second to realise it had come from him. Pulling Harper closer to him, he fixed Hans with a menacing stare. 'Back off, Langenberg.'

'Sorry, old chap.' Hans frowned. 'Didn't mean to tread on your toes.'

'It didn't stop you treading on mine.' Both men turned to look at Harper, who was stifling a giggle.

Vieri glared at her. She was drunk; she had to be. 'You, young lady, need some fresh air.' Loosening his arm, he took hold of Harper's hand. 'We are leaving.'

He started to weave his way out of the ballroom, keeping Harper's hand in a firm grip as he negotiated a path through the noisy throng of people, ignoring all attempts to stop them from leaving. They made their way down a corridor, Harper's shoes clicking on the flagstoned floor as she hurried to keep up with him, until they reached an ancient oak-panelled door, and, sliding the heavy iron bolt across, Vieri ushered them out into a secluded courtyard. It was quiet and dark out here, the music from the ballroom reduced to little more than a dull thud. High castle walls on all four sides protected them from the breeze but the air was still cold and Vieri felt Harper shiver beside him.

'Here.' Shrugging off his jacket, he draped it

over her shoulders. 'So…' He held her at arm's length. 'How much have you had to drink?'

'I don't know.' She tipped her chin. 'I wasn't counting. How much have you had?'

'For your information I am stone-cold sober.'

'Really?' Her nose wrinkled. 'How boring.' Shrugging off his jacket, she tried to give it back to him. 'I don't need this. I am used to properly cold winters. Where I come from this would be considered positively balmy.'

'Well, from where I come from it isn't and I'm not letting you get hypothermia.' He positioned the jacket over her shoulders again.

'What is it with you, bossing me around all the time?' Without waiting for an answer, Harper took a few steps away and twirled herself around, holding the lapels of the jacket across her chest. 'But thank you for bringing me here. I have actually had a lovely evening.'

He'd noticed. Vieri ground down on his jaw. But if she was baiting him, he refused to bite. 'It's Alfonso you should be thanking. It was his idea.'

'Then I will, the next time we visit. He is such a lovely man. And so generous. Everyone here thinks the world of him.'

'Yes.' Vieri's voice sounded gruff in the dim light. 'I know.'

'It is so sad to think that he is dying.' She turned mournful wide eyes in his direction.

'Everyone has to die eventually.'

'I guess.' Vieri watched as she moved to the centre of the courtyard, throwing back her head and looking up into the sky. 'When my mother died, Leah and I were told that she had become a star in the sky. We didn't really believe it, even then.' She paused, staring intently upwards. 'But on a starlit night like tonight I still find myself wondering which one she might be. Silly, I know.'

'That's not silly.' Vieri quietly closed the gap between them, coming to stand next to her. 'It's a way of remembering her.' There was a beat of silence. 'How old were you, when she died?'

'Twelve.' Harper turned to look at him.

'And it was an accident with a shotgun, you say?'

'Yes.' Her voice was very small.

'What happened?' Suddenly Vieri found he wanted to know the details. To try and understand the event that had so obviously shaped this young woman's life.

'My father was away one night, helping out on a neighbouring estate.' Vieri could see the effort it took for Harper to talk about this, even now, years after the event. 'My mother heard a disturbance, someone trying to poach the birds, so she took the shotgun to try and scare them off. It was dark, she wasn't used to handling a gun, she tripped…'

'I'm sorry.' Vieri held her gaze. 'That must have been very hard for you all.'

'Yep.' Harper touched the slender column of her throat. 'Pretty tough. She died trying to protect a few birds that were going to end up getting shot anyway. Ironic when you think about it. And Dad never forgave himself. He was convinced it was his fault.'

And she had been left to pick up the pieces. She didn't say as much, but as Vieri studied Harper's proud silhouette in the dim light it was plain to see—the care and compassion, the *responsibility*, that sat so heavily on her slender shoulders. It was clear that she would do anything for her family, even if, as he strongly suspected, they didn't appreciate her. He wondered if her father and sister had any idea how lucky they were to have her, to have a family at all, in fact. But if they were guilty of taking her for granted, where did that leave him? He was using her entirely for his own gain. It was an uncomfortable thought.

'Anyway…' she gave him a forced smile '…that's enough talk about sad things for one night. What I'd really like to do is dance.' She looked at him boldly. 'With you, I mean.'

Vieri shook his head. 'We're not going back in there.'

'Who said anything about going inside?' Removing his jacket, she held it at arm's length. 'We can dance here, under the stars.' The jacket was dropped theatrically to the ground.

'Harper…'

'Come on, it will be fun.'

Suddenly she was advancing towards him, holding out her arms invitingly. Too invitingly. The scarlet dress glowed in the dim light, the sheer fabric of the bodice pulling tight around the swell of her breasts as she closed the gap between them, positioning herself in front of him like a defiant temptress. It was a lethal combination and suddenly Vieri understood why red meant danger. A danger that increased tenfold as she slid her arms around his neck.

He managed to resist for all of two seconds. But then suddenly his arms were around her waist, and he was drawing her into his body, her bare flesh tantalisingly cold beneath his hot hands. They began to sway, Harper's softly sensual body leaning into his as their feet moved beneath them to the barely audible strains of music coming from inside.

Vieri closed his eyes, just for a moment. This felt good. *Too good.* He was already guilty of using Harper; he could not let himself take advantage of her any further. But as his hands strayed lightly over the ruched fabric of that firm little behind it was so hard to hold back. His body was already defying him, reacting wildly to the feel of her luscious body against his, the scent of her hair, the small but erotic movement as she swayed in his arms. As the tightening in his groin intensified, with supreme effort Vieri forced himself to stop.

'That's enough.' His words were harsher than he had intended, and he saw Harper's eyes widen as he roughly moved to hold her at arm's length. He meant to apologise but before he had the chance Harper had launched into an attack.

'Okay, fine, I get the message.' Smoothing down the fabric over her hips, she turned to glare at him. 'Heaven forbid that we should actually start to enjoy ourselves.'

'I think you have enjoyed yourself quite enough for one evening.'

'And you haven't, I suppose? Apart from when you took the time to glare at me, of course.'

'I'm surprised you noticed. You seemed to be far too busy throwing yourself at every available man.'

'Perhaps if you had paid me a bit more attention I wouldn't have needed to *throw myself* at anyone.' She drew in a sharp breath that pushed her breasts seductively upwards. 'You were the one who said we needed to put on a convincing performance and yet within minutes of arriving you were swanning off with your gaggle of female admirers.'

'I was merely engaging in the normal rules of social etiquette.'

'Well perhaps you should have spent more time *engaging* with the person you are actually *engaged* to.'

'I would have done, if I could have got a look in.'

'You didn't even try, Vieri.'

They glared at each other, childish hostility shimmering between them.

'So that's what all that unbecoming behaviour was about.' Keeping his tone low, Vieri gestured towards the party inside. 'You were trying to make me jealous.'

'Ha!' Harper gave a contemptuous laugh. 'I'm sorry to disappoint you and your mountainous ego but my *unbecoming* behaviour was simply me having a good time. Enjoying the company of some civilised men.'

'Civilised be damned.' Vieri's voice boomed around the courtyard. 'I saw the way Hans looked at you and there was nothing civilised about that.'

'Excuse me, you're the one who just accused me of trying to make you jealous.' Harper leapt on his words. 'But it's clear that you don't need any help in that department. You are more than capable of turning all green-eyed monster without any help from me.'

'Nonsense.'

'And while we are on the subject, what was all that chest beating in front of Hans? All that, *"Back off, Langenberg."'* She mimicked Vieri's voice, piling on a heavy Sicilian accent to perfectly capture his ill humour.

Vieri felt the blood fire through his veins. 'That's enough.' Harper was in danger of seriously overstepping the line. 'I'm taking you home.'

'And supposing I don't want to go. Supposing I want to stay and have some more fun.'

'Trust me, Harper, you don't get the choice. The fun is over.' Striding over to pick up his jacket from the ground, Vieri pointedly gave it a shake before looping his finger through the label and tossing it over his shoulder. 'We are leaving. Now!'

CHAPTER SIX

'HERE, DRINK THIS.' Vieri slid the cup of espresso coffee across the table towards her.

'For the last time, I am *not* drunk.' Harper angrily folded her arms across her chest, glaring at Vieri, who was seated on the sofa opposite her.

It was true. Maybe she had had one too many glasses of champagne at the ball—why else would she have been stupid enough to ask Vieri to dance with her? But the way he had rebuffed her, his surly silence in the car on the way back to the apartment and now his patronising refusal to believe anything she said had sobered her up nicely, thank you very much.

She probably should have gone straight to her room. That had been her intention as she had simmered beside him in the warm, purring darkness of the car. Even when they were back at the apartment, Vieri noisily making coffee, she had intended to show her defiance by sweeping past him and marching to her room, firmly closing the door behind her. But halfway there she had realised that that was actually more cowardly than agreeing to sit down and have a cup of coffee with him. That fleeing to her bedroom would send out the message that she was upset by what had happened between them. Which of course she was.

Asking him to dance had been a stupid idea; she should never have done it. But his display of possessiveness in front of Hans, and then the way he had asked about her family, the surprising tenderness in his expression, had emboldened her, made her drop her guard. Only for him to throw her foolishness back in her face by rebuffing her, shoving her away as if she was nothing, no one.

She lifted her cup to her lips, sullenly eyeing her adversary over the rim. He had pulled loose the bow tie so that it lay flat against the crisp white of his shirt, which had the top buttons undone, the sleeves rolled up to reveal dark-skinned forearms. He looked as stunningly drop-dead gorgeous as ever but there was something about him, a sharpness that stiffened his posture, tempering his usual languid style.

Perhaps he was afraid she was going to leap on him. Forget her place once again and demand that he take her to bed, make love to her. That thought did very disturbing things to her insides and she hastily swallowed a mouthful of hot coffee to try and drown them. Vieri Romano need have no fear of that. She had learned her lesson. From now on she intended to show him just how much she didn't care.

She watched as he refilled his cup. 'Well, in that case there are a couple of things I would like to discuss with you.'

'Go on.' With studied indifference, Harper arranged the scarlet folds of her dress.

'First, I thought you would like to know that your sister has turned up.'

'Leah?' Leaping to her feet, all pretence of coolness gone, Harper flew to his side, perching herself down on the sofa next to him. 'Oh, thank God.' She searched his face for information. 'Is she okay?'

'As far as I know.'

'Oh, thank God.' She repeated the words on a long exhalation of breath. 'Where is she? How did you find her?'

'She was tracked down to a casino in Atlantic City. She has been collected from those premises.'

'Collected from those premises?' Immediately alarm surged through her. It was always the same with Leah; she evoked this hugely protective instinct in Harper, as if she had been put on this earth solely to save her twin sister. Which in a way she had.

A sickly child, Leah had been diagnosed with

kidney failure shortly after their mother's death, compounding the family's distress. They were told she would need a kidney transplant and Harper was found to be the perfect match but legally they still had to wait four long years until the girls were old enough before the transplant could go ahead. But finally it had happened and Harper was able to give her sister the precious gift of a healthy life. But it did mean that she still worried obsessively over Leah, probably far more than she should.

'So what does that mean?' She cross-examined Vieri. 'You had your security guys go and pick her up?'

'Correct.'

Harper remembered the two brutes who had grabbed her in Spectrum nightclub, the way they had manhandled her when they had thought she was Leah. And they had been obeying Vieri's orders. Were they the same goons who had been sent to 'collect' Leah?

'Well, I hope they didn't hurt her. I'm telling you now, Vieri, if one of your bully-boy thugs has harmed so much as a hair on my sister's head…'

Vieri let out a low scoff. 'Forgive me if I don't appear too terrified.'

'I mean it. If any harm has come to Leah you will have me to answer to.' His sarcasm only served to fire her temper more. 'You can forget about this whole charade with your godfather. I will go right round there and tell him everything.'

'Really?' Vieri leant back into the sofa. 'And will this *everything* include how your precious sister wilfully cheated me out of thirty thousand dollars?'

Harper paused, searching for a firmer footing. 'If necessary, yes. Alfonso will understand. He is a good man. Maybe he deserves to know the truth.'

'And maybe you should think very carefully before you continue this conversation. I am not going to be held to ransom over this, Harper. You knew the score when you agreed to take on your sister's debt. Either you continue with our arrangement or you pack your bags and get the hell out of here. The choice is yours.' Dark blue eyes flashed at her. 'But rest assured, if that happens, the debt will still have to be paid.'

Harper glared at him, the blood pounding in her ears, fear and anger and frustration coursing through her body.

'Is that a threat?'

'Take it any way you want.'

'And what do you think Alfonso would make of that? The fact that you are prepared to hound two young women for a sum of money that is nothing more than a pittance to you.'

'You leave my godfather out of this.' Danger tinged Vieri's voice.

'Maybe he needs to know just what a bully and a thug you really are.'

'*Chiedo scusa*, I beg your pardon?' With a flash of anger, Vieri leant in, so close that she could feel his hot breath on her cheeks. 'What did you just call me?'

Harper swallowed hard. Perhaps she had gone too far. But stubborn pride refused to let her back down. She was too worried about Leah, and about what might happen to her if she did try and pull out of this hateful deception. She was trapped and, worse than that, trapped by a man who did the most terrible things to her. Who right now, despite everything, was firing her senses, making her body throb with need.

But if she was trapped she would fight, no matter how useless it might be, like a fox caught in one of her father's snares. Because the alternative was to give in, surrender to this man, and she would never do that.

'You heard,' she obstinately fired back.

'Indeed I did.' His voice was terrifyingly soft.

Grimly Harper hung onto her defiance. 'You don't intimidate me, Vieri.'

'No?' His gaze deliberately burned into hers, the small space between them humming with threat. 'You call me a bully and a thug and yet you are not intimidated by me. Doesn't that make you rather stupid?'

'Oh, you would love that, wouldn't you?' Still she pushed. 'For me to be scared of you.'

'On the contrary.' Reaching forward, he brushed his fingers along her jawline, before curling his hand possessively under her chin. 'What I would love would be for you to honour the clearly laid-out terms of our agreement and start behaving like my fiancée.'

'But...' His finger pressed against her lip to silence her.

'What I would really *love* would be for you to start showing me some respect.'

Harper swallowed against her closing throat. The heat of his fingers was setting her face alight, hammering her heart wildly in her chest. In theory she only had to turn her head to release his grip but somehow she couldn't do it. His punishing gaze was holding her captive and it was as much as she could do to drag in a ragged breath.

'I will start showing you some respect when I think you have earned it.' Somehow she managed to choke out some words.

'Is that right?' With a cold laugh Vieri moved his body fractionally closer. 'So tell me, just for argument's sake, what exactly *do* I have to do to earn your respect? Obviously letting you step in for your thief of a sister hasn't done the trick, despite the fact that I could so easily have gone to the police and got her into serious trouble. And then there's the time and effort I have put into finding her, not to mention giving her money and putting her on a plane back to Scotland. Clearly that is not enough.'

'I'm sorry?' Harper croaked. 'What did you just say?'

'I said that Leah is on her way back to Scotland. For your information that is what my "bully-boy thugs" have been doing. On my instructions and at my expense they have been putting your precious sister on a plane back to her homeland.' He twisted the hand that still held her chin to look at the watch on his wrist. 'She should be landing in Glasgow in a couple of hours.'

'Oh.'

'Yes, oh.'

There was a heavy pause, the air between them thickening as suddenly the swirling hostility began to morph into something much more slick and dark and dangerous. Harper could only watch, her breath caught in her throat, as Vieri let go of her chin and slid his hand around the nape of her neck, drawing her closer to him until their lips were only fractionally apart. And then they were touching.

Harper closed her eyes against the white-hot bolt of sensation that stormed through her, flooding her core. Immediately the kiss took on a life of its own, hot and damp and deeply sensual, leaving Harper no power to resist. Her lips willingly parted to allow Vieri's sweet assault, her own body responding with blind need as she pressed herself against him to feel more of his silken mouth and the raw, sexual promise beneath.

Slowly Vieri's fingers stroked upwards from the base of her neck and Harper shuddered with pleasure. Threading his fingers through her hair now, he dislodged the hairpins until her hair cascaded over her shoulders in a tumble of soft curls. Then, pulling away from her mouth, he stared at her. Harper blinked back, her heart thundering like fury. She would defy anyone to be immune to those eyes. She had no defences against their drugging power.

Gathering up a thick swathe of her hair, he twisted it so that he could hold it in his grip, tugging so that it pulled lightly against her scalp, in a blatant display of seduction and control. And then his mouth was on hers again, gloriously hot and wonderfully soft, yet firm too, like a wicked promise covered in satin.

Harper moved her arms around his neck, her fingers threading through his hair, pushing up through the thick dark waves, her nails digging into his scalp, almost to the point of pain. And

Vieri responded in kind, possessively tightening his hold on her hair so that the kiss deepened, their bodies closing together. Pinpricks of pain tingled across her scalp, heightening the wild sensation of pleasure as Vieri's free arm snaked round her waist, then up over her bare back, the flat of his palm pressing firmly between her shoulder blades.

Their mouths parted for a second, just long enough for Harper to take a gasp of breath and then he was claiming her again, pushing her back against the sofa and leaning forward to cover her body with his own.

'You drive me crazy, d'you know that?' Vieri's low voice growled hot in her ear. 'You and this damned dress have been taunting me all evening.'

'We have?'

'Yes, you have.' His growl deepened. 'Don't pretend you didn't know. Ever since I walked into your room and saw you standing there admiring yourself I have been thinking of ways to get you out of it.'

Propping himself up on one arm, he stared down at her face before lowering his head so that his hair brushed tantalisingly across the bare skin of her chest. Harper closed her eyes as the damp heat of his mouth started to trace the swell of her breasts, his lips dragging against the skin and leaving a rash of goosebumps in their wake.

'Well…' she sighed over his head '…that was never my intention.'

'No?' Vieri murmured against her. 'Well, you could have fooled me.' Raising his head, he moved his hand to the strap of her dress, sliding it slowly, seductively over her shoulder. Harper arched against his touch, her heart hammering wildly against her ribcage. 'You had every man at that ball lusting after you, Ms McDonald, as I'm sure you well know. I suspect you knew exactly what you were doing when you chose this dress.'

'Ah, but that's just it.' Her words stuttered in her throat as Vieri continued his assault, lathing his tongue into the valley between her breasts. 'I didn't choose it.'

'No?' Moving his hand to cup one swollen breast, Vieri squeezed it gently in his palm. 'Then who did? I feel I should thank them.' He altered his position so that he settled his groin against hers, the shockingly hard evidence of his arousal shooting arrows of lust through Harper.

'It was someone I met by chance in the boutique.' She croaked the words.

'Oh, yes?'

'Yes. She knows you, as a matter of fact. She said you wouldn't like the dress I had originally chosen.'

'Interesting. Who is this mystery woman with impeccable taste?'

'Umm, I can't tell you. I've just remembered I'm not supposed to say.'

'Then I can see I am going to have to think of a way to prise the information out of you. Now, let me see…' He paused, his eyes flitting darkly over her heated face, over the swell of her breasts that rose and fell with each ragged breath. 'Where shall I start?'

His fingers slid under the bodice of her dress, releasing her breasts. For a moment he just stared at her, his eyes full of hunger, and Harper's nipples, already almost unbearably hard, tightened still further. Then his hands reached to cup her breasts and he held their swollen weight with such care, such obvious appreciation, it was all she could do to stop herself from whimpering with pleasure.

He lowered his head until his mouth was only a fraction away from one breast, his hot, silky breath caressing her skin until slowly, very slowly, he took the puckered nipple in his mouth. Now Harper did moan, a blissful, guttural sound, coming from somewhere deep in the back of her throat. And as Vieri started to rasp his tongue over her aching peak, stopping only to suck again, to repeat his deliriously wonderful assault, Harper's hands flew to the back of his head, holding him tightly against her, desperate for this torturous pleasure never to stop.

But eventually he moved, his head coming back up, a half-smile twisting his mouth. 'Am I any nearer to breaking your code of silence? If not I am more than happy to continue.'

Please, yes. Harper screamed the words inside her head. He was teasing her, she knew that; he didn't give a damn about who had picked out her dress. They were playing a game here but she had no idea what the rules were. Only that Vieri had made them up, that everything was on his terms. It felt forbidden, dangerous, and as if it was only going to end one way. Badly. But it also felt wildly exciting, exhilarating, like nothing she had ever experienced before. And deep down, somewhere inside that sex-befuddled brain of hers, she knew she would never have the strength to make it stop. She had no alternative but to play along.

'I'll give you a clue.' She arched her back, jutting her chest forward, inviting him to take her once more. 'She is almost related to you.'

Vieri frowned, then dipped his head again. 'Well, that is going to be difficult.' His hand cupped her other breast, his tongue delicately tracing the outline of her nipple. 'Seeing as I have no living relatives. Not that I'm aware of anyway.' Slowly his mouth closed around her nipple and Harper let herself surrender to the pleasure.

'Think of your godfather, then.'

'Alfonso?' He abandoned her breast long

enough to say the name, returning to muffle the next sentence against it. 'What does he have to do with it?'

'Because it was his niece, Donatella!'

'Donatella?'

His reaction to her name was extreme—brutal. As if venom had somehow entered his bloodstream, his body went suddenly rigid, his head jerking back to expose the strong column of his neck.

'Y...yes.' Stuttering with surprise, Harper could only stare up at him in astonishment.

'You are telling me that Donatella Sorrentino chose this dress for you?'

'Yes. Why, does it matter?'

His reply was a violent oath in a foreign tongue. Releasing her shoulders, he leapt to his feet, for a second glaring down at her dishevelled body with undisguised hatred burning in his eyes. Then turning, he moved as if he was desperate to get away from her.

Harper stared at the broad expanse of his back in total shock. She could see the bunched muscles of his biceps flexing as he folded his arms in front of him, his shoulder blades jutted rigidly beneath the fine fabric of his shirt.

She pulled her eyes away, looking down at herself with distress, horror even. Her breasts were fully exposed, still tingling from where Vieri's mouth had been, her nipples hard and throbbing. Snatching up the strap of the dress, she pulled it back over her shoulder, struggling to tuck herself back into the tight bodice. And only just in time.

Vieri swung back round to look at her again, resentment scoring his face, as if he had somehow hoped she had disappeared while his back was turned.

'You need to go to bed.' It was an order, a cruel dismissal, his blue-black eyes still alight with fury.

Harper certainly wasn't going to challenge him. She couldn't get away fast enough. Leaping off the sofa, she snatched up the skirt of her dress and swept past him, heading for her rooms as fast as she could, marching through her dressing room and into her bedroom and slamming the door behind her. Only then did she let herself breathe, leaning back against the door, slowly sliding down until she was crouched on the floor in a puddle of red satin. Only then did she let herself surrender to the misery and injustice of it all, to the painful burn of tears that blocked her throat.

CHAPTER SEVEN

'NEED ANY COMPANY?'

Vieri tightened his grip around the tumbler of whisky in his hand. He growled his negative reply, leaving the heavily perfumed female hovering beside him no room for doubt. The only company he wanted right now was the alcohol in his glass and the hope that enough of it would numb his murderous thoughts.

He had chosen this dingy bar, in a far from salubrious area of Palermo, because he didn't want to talk to anyone, didn't want to see anyone. Signalling to the barman to refill his glass, he took another deep slug of whisky, returning the glass to the sticky bar top with a thud. He'd drink this and then he'd go. Being here was doing nothing to improve his state of mind and he could already feel the beginnings of an alcohol-induced headache starting to thrum at his temples.

Donatella Sorrentino. He repeated her name in his head, feeling his muscles tighten, his skin crawl. The idea that she was here, somewhere in Palermo, at the same time as him filled him with a bitter loathing that refused to abate. He imagined that he could feel her evil presence all around him, even though he knew she would never frequent a place like this. But like a rat in a sewer she was there, unseen, a dark, malevolent presence.

Presumably she was back in Palermo because she had heard about Alfonso and was circling the water like a predatory shark. Well, she was going to be sorely disappointed. She might be Alfonso's niece, his only living relative, but, as his godfather's executor, Vieri knew for a fact that she wasn't going to get a cent of his inheritance. The entire estate was to be divided between the many charities he supported. Alfonso had disowned his niece long ago, on the night his brother had been gunned down in the street—the night Donatella hadn't so much as shed a tear for her father.

It disgusted Vieri to think that he could ever have been taken in by that woman. That he could have gone to bed with her, made love to her, planned a future with her. Blind to her faults, he had still been pining for her even after she had so unceremoniously dumped him. But discovering her final act of treachery had changed all that. And his misplaced devotion had turned into a heavy, poisonous weight that had sat inside him ever since.

He had only found out the truth by accident. Months after he and Donatella had gone their separate ways, Vieri had been dating a local girl when she had let slip that her sister was a nurse in a private clinic and that Donatella Sorrentino had been in for a termination. With a tidal wave of fury Vieri had known, right at that very moment, that the child had been his. Dates had been demanded, his poor unsuspecting girlfriend left with no choice but to extract the details from her sister. And they fitted perfectly. The child was his. Without even mentioning it to him, Donatella Sorrentino had had an abortion, terminated his child. A child that would have been the only family he had ever had.

Thanks to Alfonso, he had never had the chance to exact his revenge. Instead of tracking down Donatella with a view to God knew what, he had been put on a flight to New York, forced to concentrate on making a new life for himself. And now, of course, he was very grateful for that. He hadn't laid eyes on Donatella since the day she had told him their affair was over. But the thought of her here, in Palermo, filled him with a towering rage. And the idea that she had chosen Harper's dress, come anywhere near her, in fact, exploded white lights behind his eyes.

Swirling the last of the liquor around in his glass, Vieri swallowed it in one gulp. It wasn't helping. It couldn't erase the thought of that evil woman tainting his Harper. *His Harper?* Where had that come from? Since when had he started to think of Harper McDonald as *his*? He drummed his fingers on the bar top. But there was no denying that Harper filled his thoughts more and more, that something about her, *everything about her*, made her impossible to ignore. Not just in a sexual way, although that was a powerful force, but in a more deep-rooted emotional way that was totally unfamiliar to him. A way that he didn't want to examine.

Vieri put his head in his hands. This evening had been a disaster. His plan had been to let Harper enjoy the ball, then take her back to the apartment, soften her up by telling her that Leah was safe and well and then hit her with the fact that their 'arrangement' had been changed. That they were, in fact, going to have to get married. Vieri suspected that Harper wouldn't take the news well, as indeed he hadn't, but there was no alternative. They were in too deep. This was going to have to happen and somehow they had to deal with it.

But the plan had started to unravel very early on, triggered by seeing those predatory men's hands all over Harper on the dance floor. And taking her out to the courtyard hadn't helped, his control slipping dangerously when faced with the fierce temptation of her seductively sexy body. He had just about managed to keep a hold of himself and get her back to the apartment when they had started to argue, any ideas he had had of coaxing her into compliance replaced by bitter recriminations, macho chest-beating and veiled threats. It was not the way he had intended it to go. Especially when, on hearing himself telling her she could pack her bags and leave, the strangest sensation had crept over him. A sort of hollow emptiness, a panic almost, at the thought of losing her. It had come out of nowhere, that acute sense of loss, of abandonment. And the worst of it was, he knew it had nothing whatever to do with their 'arrangement' and everything to do with the way he was starting to feel about her. The way she had got to him.

Something that had been all too evident when he had given in to the thundering in his head and started to kiss her. One minute he had been incensed by the totally unjustified way she'd been laying into him and the next that fiery defiance was turning him on like a tap on full pressure. Somehow her incredible sexiness had got to him, hot-wired his libido into life until all he'd been able to think about was taking her in his arms and making love to her. Making her sweet body his.

And then she had mentioned Donatella. Vieri recalled her stunned expression when he had pushed her away, the hurt and pain that had been drawn across her face before she had collected herself, finally sweeping past him to the sanctuary of her room.

A couple of whisky-soaked hours had passed since then, but the memory still made Vieri grind down hard on his jaw. She hadn't deserved that, the cruelly dismissive way he had treated her. He shouldn't have taken out his seething anger for Donatella on her.

But maybe it was for the best. Throwing a handful of notes onto the bar, he rose unsteadily from the stool. For Harper's sake they needed to keep their relationship professional, businesslike. Anything else, no matter how tempting, would just complicate matters, muddy the waters. He needed to protect her, against himself, because he couldn't bear for her to get hurt. And that was what would happen if she tried to get close to him. Because he was emotionally sterile, he had nothing to give her. Donatella had seen to that.

It occurred to him that in a funny sort of way she had done him a favour by turning up, interfering in Harper's choice of dress. If she hadn't, the evening might well have ended in a very different way; it had certainly been heading rapidly down that path. He could have been in bed with Harper now, making love to her, maybe even for the second or third time. Because Vieri already knew that once with Harper would never be enough. Yes, it was just as well they had parted when they did.

Pushing open the door of the bar, he stumbled out, the cold air hitting his face, sobering him up. Shoving his hands into the pockets of his trousers he set off in search of a taxi to take him home. The fact was, Harper McDonald was too good for him. He gave a gruff laugh into the night air. And that was something he had never imagined saying about any woman, ever.

'Harper? Is that you?' Harper had never, *ever* been so glad to hear her sister's sleep-muffled voice.

'Yes, Leah, it's me.'

Awake for most of the night, Harper had been waiting for the hours to slowly drag by before she could finally call home. She had held her breath as the phone rang, willing her sister to answer it, terrified that she wasn't there, that somehow she had gone missing again.

'What time is it?' Leah whispered groggily.

'It's nearly seven a.m. in Sicily.'

'Sicily?' This cut through the fog of sleep.

'Yes, that's where I am, Leah. In Sicily.'

'What on earth are you doing there?'

'What *on earth* do you think I'm doing here?' Somewhere in amongst the massive relief that

Leah was safe, Harper felt a surge of anger. 'I'm clearing up your mess, of course.' She gripped her phone tightly to her ear. 'How could you do it, Leah? How could you disappear with thirty thousand dollars of Vieri Romano's money?'

'Oh.' Harper could perfectly picture her sister's guilty face. 'You know about that?'

'Of course I know about that. That's why I'm here, repaying your debt.'

'But how? I mean, I don't understand.'

'When you disappeared without a trace, thanks for that by the way, I had to go looking for you. I went to Spectrum...'

'You flew to New York?'

'No, I swam. Of course I bloody flew to New York.' Harper took in a breath. 'I was manhandled by Vieri's henchmen because they thought I was you, then delivered to the great man himself, only to be told, once he'd established who I was, that you had scarpered with his money.'

'Oh, God, Harper. I'm so sorry.'

'So you should be. But frankly sorry isn't going to cut it. So come on, then, I'm waiting. Why the hell did you do it?'

There was a pause on the other end of the phone.

'It's a bit of a long story.'

'I thought it might be.'

'I met this guy, Max Rodriguez.' Leah started

tentatively. 'He was a bar manager at Spectrum but he was also a professional gambler. He said if I gave him the thirty thousand he could double it, maybe even triple it, in just one night.'

'And you believed him?'

'He was really convincing, Harper.'

'And it didn't occur to you to wonder why, if he was such a whizz at the gaming tables, he still needed to work in the bar of a nightclub?'

'Not really.'

'Honestly, Leah!'

'It's all very well for you to scoff now, with the benefit of hindsight. But at the time it seemed like an excellent plan. I thought I could repay Vieri, then send the rest of the money back home, take some of the pressure off you and Dad.'

'How very kind.' Harper kept the sarcasm in her voice but she could feel her anger starting to melt. This was typical of Leah, to get involved in a stupid, crazy scheme that brought nothing but trouble for those all around her, especially herself, but only because she was trying to help. Generous to a fault, and she had plenty of those, Leah did all the wrong things for the right reasons. 'So what went wrong with this brilliant plan?'

'Max lost the money.' She sounded genuinely crestfallen. 'Every last cent. I'd gone with him, to this casino in Atlantic City. Obviously I wasn't going to let him just take my money without me being there to make sure he didn't just run off with it.'

'Obviously.'

'But after he'd lost the money he did a disappearing act. I ended up having to stay on at the casino, working in the kitchens to cover the drinks bill he'd run up, pay for the suite of rooms he'd booked, all using my money.'

'Technically I think it was Vieri's money.'

'Well, yes.'

'But you're okay?' Harper's anxiety spiked. 'I mean, they didn't treat you badly?'

'No. The staff at the casino were decent enough, given the circumstances. But owing Mr Romano thirty thousand dollars was bad enough in itself.'

'Oh, Leah. Why didn't you ring me?'

'Because I was ashamed, I guess. Because I'd messed up yet again. I think I was hoping I would somehow get the money to repay him and no one need ever know anything about it.'

'And how, exactly, were you going to do that?'

'I don't know. Rob a bank, marry a rich man, sell my body to the highest bidder?'

'Leah!'

'I had no idea, Harper, beyond going into hiding and getting as many jobs as I could and saving like hell so that I could at least start to pay some of the money back. I was being trained to work in the casino, on the tables, when Vieri's goons burst in and bundled me into a limo. I had no idea where we were going. Turned out to be the nearest airport.'

'But whatever were you thinking?' Harper moved the phone to her other ear. 'Even if by some miracle you hadn't lost all the money, what about the original deal you had made with Vieri?'

'I was going to pay him back his money and then pull out. I knew I'd have to look for a job somewhere else, but I figured it would be worth it.'

'Didn't you care about letting him down?'

'Oh, come on, Harper. You don't feel sorry for men like Vieri Romano! It was a stupid idea anyway.'

'Yeah, a stupid idea that I now have to see through.'

'So is that what you're doing in Sicily?' Leah breathed into the phone. 'Honouring my agreement?'

'Yes, Leah. That's exactly what I'm doing.'

'*You* are pretending to be engaged to Vieri Romano?' She had the nerve to laugh.

'I said so, didn't I?' Harper bristled with annoyance. 'I'm glad you find it so hilarious.'

'No, not hilarious.' Leah steadied herself. 'I'm just surprised, that's all.'

'What, surprised that I'm having to pick up the pieces of your shattered life yet again?'

There was silence from the other end of the phone.

'I'm sorry, Lea.' Instantly Harper regretted her sharp tongue. 'I didn't mean it like that.'

'Yes, you did.' Leah let out a deep sigh. 'And you're right. We both know that I owe you everything. And all I want is to try and make it up to you.'

'How many times? You don't need to make anything up to me. Especially if it means coming up with hare-brained schemes like becoming engaged to billionaire Sicilian businessmen.'

She was relieved to hear her sister laugh.

'Okay, point taken. But at least I can sort this mess out myself. If you can book me a flight to Sicily—I'd do it myself except I have literally no money—then we can swap places and you can come home.'

'No, Leah.'

'But why not? It's the obvious solution.'

'Because it's way too late for that. I've been introduced to people, got to know his godfather. And besides, Vieri would never agree to it. Your name is mud as far as he is concerned.'

'But we look so alike. He probably wouldn't even notice the difference.'

'Trust me, he would notice.'

Harper bit down on her lip. She had answered too quickly, given herself away.

'So, you and Vieri…' Leah probed quietly.
'Have you got close?'

'No.'

'Oh, my God, you have, haven't you? You have
fallen for him!'

'No! Of course I haven't!'

'Oh, Harps, be careful. I mean, I know he's a
complete hunk with enough sex appeal to deci-
mate a small planet, but even so, a man like Vieri
Romano… He breaks hearts for a living.'

'I have not fallen for Vieri Romano! He's an
arrogant, overbearing egotist. Why ever would I
fall for a man like that?'

'I don't know. You tell me.' Her voice was laced
with amusement.

'Look, Leah, I'm not going to discuss this any
further. We need to make plans for the next few
weeks.'

'I suspect you've already done that.'

'I'm being serious, Leah. I'm not sure when I'm
going to get back to Glenruie, but in the mean-
time you are in charge. How is Dad? Have you
seen him?'

'Not yet. It was late when I got in last night.
The kitchen looked in a bit of a state.'

'I can imagine. You are going to have to be
tough with him, you know.'

'I know.'

'And I'm down to do quite a few shifts at the

Lodge. I was going to ring and cancel them but now you're back you can do them for me. They're all written on the calendar.'

'Okay, fine.' She sighed heavily. 'Why does it feel as if I've drawn the short straw?'

'Don't even go there, Leah!' Harper gave a brisk laugh. 'Look, I'm going to have to go now. So glad you are safe, sis.'

'Thanks. And sorry…you know…'

'Forget it.'

'Love you, sis.'

'You too.'

Ending the call, Harper moved over to the window. Dawn was just beginning to break over the city, the rising sun defining the jagged black mountains in the distance, picking out the orange brickwork of the chaotic conglomeration of houses below.

It was so beautiful here, and yet Harper had never felt more isolated, more alone. The torture of what had happened between her and Vieri the evening before had robbed her of a night's sleep and still coursed shamefully through her veins. The way she had responded to his touch, been so near to giving herself to him, exposing her feelings, now scored her cheeks with humiliation. One minute she had been melting beneath the seductive power of his mouth and the next he had cruelly dismissed her, brutally reminding her of who was in charge. He pulled her strings and she danced. He cut them and she fell.

Turning away from the window, she went back and sat on the edge of the bed, bunching the bedcover between her fingers. It had been the mention of that Donatella woman that had thrown him into a rage—clearly something had gone on between the two of them. Was it possible they had been lovers? Were they *still* lovers? The thought cut through her like a blade. Sucking in a breath, she made herself focus on the reality of her situation. Whoever Vieri saw, whatever he did, was none of her business. Their engagement was only for a few, short weeks. She just had to wrap up her emotions and get through this. Although the fact that their arrangement would only end because of Alfonso's death was something Harper had yet to come to terms with.

But when the inevitable happened she would go back to Scotland and get on with her life and put this whole, crazy episode behind her. It would be as if Vieri had never existed. And somehow, her poor virgin heart would have to find a way to heal itself.

Pulling back the feather-light duvet, she slipped underneath and curled herself into a tight ball. And finally sleep came.

CHAPTER EIGHT

A SERIES OF loud raps on her bedroom door saw Harper burrowing out of the duvet, blinking against the light.

'Harper!' There was no mistaking the deeply sonorous voice.

'Yes,' she croaked back, fumbling for her phone to see what the time was. Ten-thirty? How could that be? But before she had the chance to order her thoughts Vieri was striding into her bedroom, full of his usual command.

'You need to get up.'

Harper pushed herself up against the pillows, brushing the hair out of her eyes with a shaky hand. By the look on Vieri's face, something was wrong.

'What's the matter? What's happened?'

'I have received a message from Alfonso's nurse.' Vieri's voice was tight. 'We need to get over there right away.'

'Oh, no!' Harper felt her heart lurch. 'Alfonso...

he hasn't…? She pulled back the covers, scrambling to get out of bed.

'No, no. It's Maria. Some sort of family emergency, apparently. She has had to leave.'

'Oh, thank goodness.' Harper gave a huge sigh of relief. 'Not that I don't feel sorry for Maria, of course.' She stopped, suddenly aware of Vieri's cool blue eyes raking over her. She was wearing a pair of old fleecy tartan pyjamas, perfect for keeping out the winter chill back home, but, judging by Vieri's expression, not the sort of female night attire he was familiar with.

She gazed at him, desperately trying to ignore the stutter of her heart. Wearing faded, low-slung jeans and a grey sweatshirt, he was more casually dressed than usual, but no less devastatingly attractive. The dark shadow that shaded his jawline gave him a feral, untamed look, and his ruffled hair, that didn't appear to have been brushed any time recently, only made him seem all the more dangerously tempting. Harper bit down on her lip. Maybe this unkempt look meant he had had a bad night too. After the way he had treated her, she couldn't help but hope so.

'So, what's the plan?' She tried to sound normal, running a hand over her own sleep-tangled hair and tucking it behind her ears. But all the time she was acutely conscious of Vieri's unwavering stare. 'Can you hire a temporary nurse?'

'Already done. But Alfonso is being difficult. It seems that he wants you there.'

'Oh.' Harper nodded. 'Well, I'll get dressed and we can head straight over there.'

'I mean he wants you to move in with him.' Vieri hesitated. 'Until Maria gets back.'

'I see.' Harper bit back her surprise. 'Well, that's okay. I can do that.' Already her affection for Alfonso was such that she would do anything for him.

'Obviously I will accompany you.'

Obviously. Harper felt her stomach twist with nervous apprehension. All brisk businesslike command, there was no trace of the Vieri of last night. Of the seductive lover who had so easily smashed through her fragile defences, or the angry stranger that had followed. It occurred to her that she had no idea at all what went on in this man's head.

'Maria doesn't know how long she will have to be away,' Vieri continued. 'Do you have any commitments, at home, I mean?'

This took Harper aback. It was the first time Vieri had even mentioned the life she had had to put on hold for him.

'Actually I spoke to Leah this morning.' She fiddled with the hem of her pyjama top. 'She's safely back in Glenruie and she has agreed to do my shifts at Craigmore Lodge for me. And look after Dad.'

Vieri gave a brief nod.

'She explained to me what had happened, about the money, Vieri. How that man gambled it all away and then disappeared.' Harper took a tentative step towards him. 'Leah didn't deliberately set out to steal from you, you know. She intended to pay you back.' For some reason she felt she had to try and clear her sister's name.

'It makes no difference to me either way.' Vieri looked profoundly unconvinced, his profile set hard in silhouette against the window. 'As far as I am concerned the matter is closed. Once our arrangement has been concluded, of course.'

'Of course.' Harper chewed the inside of her lip. What was the point of even trying to get through to this man? She sighed heavily.

'We will leave in twenty minutes.'

'Fine.'

She watched as his broad-shouldered frame turned and left the room. Heading for the bathroom, she stripped off her pyjamas and stepped under the shower, hoping that the thundering water would drown out her sense of foreboding.

It seemed that no matter how hard she tried to protect herself, the web she was caught in was tightening all the time. Somehow, Vieri's control over her life was becoming more and more inescapable.

* * *

'*Benvenuto*, welcome.' Alfonso stretched out a skinny arm towards Harper, taking her hand and patting it with his own. 'Thank you so much for coming to save me in my hour of need.'

'It's nothing, Alfonso.' Harper leant in to kiss his papery cheek. 'It will be a pleasure to stay here and look after you until Maria returns.'

'You are very kind but I know what an imposition it must be for you. And for Vieri.' He shot Vieri a look. 'But I hope you will forgive the selfishness of a very old man.'

'There is nothing to forgive, Alfonso.' Vieri gave his godfather a hug, the reality of how frail Alfonso had become gripping his heart.

'Harper, my dear.' Alfonso turned to where Harper still stood beside his chair. 'Perhaps you would like to go and check your room? My housekeeper has made it ready for you but I want to make sure everything is just as you want it before she leaves for the day.'

'I'm sure it will be perfect.'

'Even so.' He touched her hand again. 'It would put my mind at rest.'

'Very well, I'll go and unpack.'

Both men watched as she left the room.

'Come and sit down, my son.' Alfonso patted the chair beside him, speaking in his native Sicilian. 'You are making me anxious, standing there with that forbidding look on your face. I hope this situation…' he waved his hand around expressively '…isn't inconveniencing you too much.'

'Not at all, *padrino*.' Vieri seated himself in a high-backed chair.

'Then what? You look troubled.'

Vieri took in a breath. 'Did you know that Donatella is back in Palermo?' He could feel a vein pulsing in his neck at the very mention of her name.

'Ah, yes, I did hear as much.'

'And that doesn't worry you?'

'Not in the least. She knows better than to show her face here.'

'But she will still try and make trouble,' Vieri replied. 'You can bet on that.'

'Donatella Sorrentino will only make trouble if we let her, Vieri. And I have no intention of doing any such thing.'

Vieri bit down hard on his jaw. Alfonso was right. Hadn't he already let her do just that by reacting so violently when he'd found out she had chosen Harper's dress? He had played right into her vicious hands.

Taking a breath, he strode over to the window, gazing out at the calm vista.

'Let it go, Vieri.' Alfonso's soft voice spoke behind him. 'That woman may have blighted your past, but don't let her blight your future.'

Vieri turned and the two men locked eyes, the air thick with words that weren't spoken. So wise, so caring—it worried Vieri considerably that Alfonso's view of his future was built on a construct of lies and deceit. It worried him, too, that his rosy picture would never happen. But it was too late for regrets. He had started this stupid charade, he had no choice but to see it through.

Harper sat down heavily on the bed. *Her* side of the bed. The housekeeper had left after Harper had insisted that the room was perfect, that there was nothing more she needed. But even though the room was perfect, the reality of the situation was far from it. Because it was evident that Harper wasn't going to be the sole occupant of this bedroom. She would be sharing it with Vieri.

She looked around in dismay. At the two sets of towels on the bed, the two white dressing gowns on the back of the door. Sharing Vieri's enormous hotel penthouse apartment had been bad enough. How on earth was she going to cope with sharing a bedroom—a bed? No, it couldn't happen! Somehow the sleeping arrangements would have to be changed.

Two pairs of eyes turned in her direction as she walked back into the salon. Alfonso gestured to her to come forward. 'I hope everything was to your satisfaction?'

'Yes, *our* room is lovely.' She ground out the words, flashing Vieri a pointed stare.

'*Bene, bene.* I thought you would like it. That bed is very special, you know. It's known as a marriage bed, hundreds of years old, I believe. Superstition has it that the couple that lie in that bed will soon be granted the blessing of a child.' His dark eyes twinkled. 'Although I suspect they may need to do more than just lie in it.'

'Alfonso!' Vieri rested his hand on his godfather's shoulder.

'Forgive me. But in my situation you can't blame me for trying to speed things up a bit. I'm not old-fashioned enough to think you have to wait to be married these days to share a bed.'

Harper sat down on the sofa, tightly crossing her legs. How awkward was this?

'Speaking of which, have you set a date yet?'

'A date?' She frowned at Alfonso, her mind still whirring with the sleeping arrangements.

'Yes.' Alfonso sat forward in his chair. 'I asked Vieri if you would be so kind as to make the wedding soon. So that I might be able to attend.'

'The w-wedding?' She shot a horrified glance at Vieri, who steadfastly refused to meet her eyes. Instead he addressed his godfather.

'We haven't had the chance to discuss it yet, *padrino.*'

'No? Well, there's no time like the present.'

Clearly Alfonso wasn't going to be deterred. 'Why don't we sort it out now? Harper, pass me my diary, will you? It's in the top drawer of my desk.'

As if in a trance, Harper did as she was told, crossing the room to retrieve Alfonso's diary and placing it in his outstretched hand.

'*Grazie*, thank you, my dear. Now let me see.' His shaky hands started to turn over the pages. 'Ah, now how about this week?' He turned the diary around, holding open the pages. Vieri and Harper peered at it. Harper's heart stopped. It was a mere two weeks away. 'Shall we say the twenty-third?'

'The twenty-third?' To Harper's horror, Vieri appeared to be considering it, worse, drawing her in. 'I think that might be possible. What do you say, Harper?'

There was a lot she wanted to say. *An awful lot.* But trapped between Alfonso's hopeful gaze and Vieri's shuttered calm she didn't know where to begin.

'I think that may be a little soon.' Her voice was tight with suppressed tension. 'Weddings take some time to organise, I believe.'

'Sadly time is not something I have a lot of.' Alfonso smiled weakly at her. 'As you know.'

Harper bit down hard on her lip. How was she supposed to counter that?

'What sort of wedding do you have in mind?'

Alfonso continued unabashed. 'Do you envisage a lavish affair?'

'No!' Harper swallowed. Five minutes ago she hadn't had any sort of wedding in mind. 'Not at all.'

'Well, I don't think a small, intimate gathering will be difficult to organise. And finding a venue certainly won't be a problem. Vieri owns several luxury hotels in Sicily alone. In fact, I have a better idea.' He pushed himself upright. 'Why don't you get married here? In the *castello* chapel. You would be doing me the greatest honour.'

'That is very kind of you, Alfonso. But all the arrangements, the disruption, will it not be too much for you?' Harper fired a surreptitious glare at Vieri. Why was he not putting a stop to this nonsense right now?

'Not at all. It will give me something to look forward to. So, is that settled, then? Saturday the twenty-third.'

Harper found herself nodding weakly.

'*Eccellente.*' Alfonso gave them both a beaming smile. 'Now, if you will call that new nurse of mine, I think it's time I took a nap.'

'And just when, *exactly*, were you going to tell me about this wedding?'

Shaking with outrage, Harper turned on Vieri as they stepped outside into the cool air.

'Keep your voice down.' Linking his arm through hers, Vieri moved them away from the *castello*. 'Getting hysterical is not going to help anyone.'

'I think I have every right to be hysterical!' Balling her hands into fists, Harper dug them further into her coat pockets. The shock of what she had just agreed to was still ringing in her ears, and having Vieri locked beside her, his towering, powerful body controlling her steps as they moved through the gardens, was doing nothing to calm her down. 'How could you have told Alfonso we would be getting married without even *asking* me first?'

'I intended to explain the situation.' Vieri stared straight ahead, his proud profile showing nothing in the way of remorse as he moved them along the gravel pathway in the direction of the formal gardens. 'But Alfonso got in there first.'

Explain the situation! Was that all he thought he had to do? Harper could hardly believe the man's arrogance. She wanted to scream and shout, to beat her fists against his conceited, iron-hard chest, but she knew she had to concentrate on the practicalities. She fought to hold her voice steady. 'This is *not* what I signed up for, Vieri. This is *not* part of the deal!'

'I appreciate that.' He walked them under the archway of the brick wall and into the formal gardens. 'I realise that the terms of our agreement will need to be renegotiated.'

'Renegotiated?' Harper brought them to a sudden stop. 'Do you really think that's all there is to it?' Her eyes flashed with fire. 'Do you really think I will agree to marry you, just like that, without you even having the courtesy to ask me?'

'Unless I am mistaken, it would seem you have already agreed.' Vieri met her blazing temper with cold, calculating eyes.

With the blood boiling in her veins, Harper didn't trust herself to speak. Because he was right, of course. She had already consented to this wedding. Acknowledging her silence with a single quirk of his dark brow, Vieri pulled her closer to him, tucking her arm against the warmth of his body as he moved them on again, between the towering box topiary. Reaching a stone bench, he released her and waited for her to sit down before seating himself beside her.

'Look, Harper, this wedding was not my idea but we can make it work.' His voice was low, confident. 'I know how fond you are of Alfonso. I know you would do anything to make his final weeks happy.' She could feel him scanning her grim profile, sense how sure he was of himself. Of her. Because, of course, she would do anything for Alfonso. Including marrying this darkly dangerous man.

'Financially I will make it worth your while,' he continued smoothly. 'You will be fully recompensed for your inconvenience.'

'I don't want your money!' Leaping to her feet, Harper rounded on him. 'And having to marry you is not an *inconvenience*. It's a total nightmare!'

She turned away, biting down on her lip to try and stop it from trembling. That had come out all wrong, had revealed far too much. Somehow her thin veil of protection had slipped, revealing her dangerously turbulent feelings beneath.

'Not necessarily.' Behind her she heard Vieri get to his feet, his voice infuriatingly calm.

'No?' She spun around. 'How can you say that? This whole thing has got completely out of hand. Quite apart from the marriage, you do realise that Alfonso expects us to share a bedroom while we are staying at the *castello*?'

'I gathered as much.' Vieri's intense stare found hers, the memory of last night after the ball, of what had so nearly happened between them, shining in their deep blue depths.

'So what exactly do you intend to do about that?' Harper hurriedly tried to suppress the fresh flutter of panic in her chest.

Vieri's mouth twitched before he finally spoke. 'I will sort it out. If that's what you want.'

'Of course it's what I want!'

'Fine.' He raised his hand dismissively, as if the matter was of no consequence, as if she was somehow being unreasonable. 'There are more than enough rooms in this *castello* for us both to have our own personal space. Alfonso need never know about our sleeping arrangements.'

'Well, see that it happens.' She threw back her head, then had to steady herself, suddenly feeling dizzy with the madness of it all.

'Are you okay?' Vieri immediately noticed the pallor of her face. 'It's cold out here. Perhaps we should go back inside.'

'No.' She dug in her heels. 'I'm going nowhere.'

'Then let me at least warm you up.' Suddenly he had gathered her in his arms, pulling her against the strong, muscled heat of his body.

For a second Harper let herself be held, her eyes closed in blissful surrender until the yearning for what could never be saw her struggle to release herself.

'Actually I would like to be left on my own.' She moved a step away and sat down heavily on the stone bench. 'I need to think things through.'

'As you wish.' But he sat down beside her again. What part of *alone* did he not understand? Several highly charged seconds of silence rolled by.

'Harper?' He rested his hand on her thigh, the heat of his palm branding her skin through the fabric of her dress.

'What?' She deliberately moved to dislodge his hand.

'I do understand that this is a big thing I am asking of you.' He closed the gap between them until his thigh was pressed against hers. She could feel the warmth radiating off him, see his soft breath in the air. 'But it doesn't have to be such an ordeal. Alfonso knows that we are only getting married so quickly for his benefit, so he will understand if it's a very private affair.'

'But we will still be married in the eyes of the law.'

'Yes, this is true. But when Alfonso…when the time comes, the marriage can be annulled.'

He had thought this all through, hadn't he? And for some reason, that only made his calculated deceit, both to his godfather and to her, seem even worse.

'However, if you decide that you can't go through with it, then I will respect that decision. I will go in there and tell Alfonso the truth, this afternoon, as soon as he awakes from his nap. You will be free to go. You need never see him again.'

Harper felt her heart plummet. The thought of not even saying goodbye to Alfonso was unthinkable. But then so was the idea of confessing that they had lied to him, that the whole engagement was a sham. He would be so disappointed. No, more than that, he would be devastated. Harper knew she could never do that to him.

She dragged in a breath of cold air to steady herself.

'Okay, I will do it.' She forced herself to meet Vieri's midnight stare. 'For Alfonso's sake, because I can't bear to think of him upset, I will agree to marry you.'

'Thank you.' Taking hold of her hand, Vieri squeezed her cold fingers in his firm, warm grasp. 'I do appreciate it.' He rose to his feet, dropping her hand but still holding her eyes. 'I will see to the arrangements right away.'

He turned, his job obviously done, and began to stride purposefully back towards the *castello*.

Harper watched his retreating figure, so tall and imposing. So unmistakeably Vieri. This impossible, arrogant, gloriously perfect specimen of manhood who had turned her life upside down. Who drove her completely crazy in every possible way. And from whom, no matter how short their so-called marriage might be, whatever might happen in the future, she feared she would never fully recover.

CHAPTER NINE

THE NEXT TWO weeks passed in a dizzying daze. Preparations for the wedding were rapidly organised, Vieri taking charge, the way he always did. And even though he did consult her, asking her opinion over some of the details, the flowers for the chapel, the food for the wedding breakfast, Harper didn't have the heart to get involved. So in the end she left it all to him.

A small guest list was drawn up, mostly comprising a few of Alfonso's trusted colleagues associated with his charities and a handful of old friends. 'There are so few of us left,' he had mournfully stated as he had turned the pages of his address book. 'That's what comes of being so ancient.'

Vieri had only invited one guest, a Sicilian friend called Jaco Valentino, someone he had known since childhood, apparently. Even that had been Alfonso's doing, casually mentioning that it would be nice to see Jaco again and why didn't Vieri see if he was free that day. Vieri had been left with no option but to agree.

Harper, herself, had no intention of inviting anybody, despite Alfonso's obvious surprise and concern that her father wouldn't be attending. She had explained, as best she could, that it would be too difficult for Angus to get away at such short notice. This, at least, was partly true. His job as gamekeeper on the Craigmore estate did make it very difficult for him to take any time off. The fact that he had absolutely no idea that his daughter was actually getting married, she kept to herself.

And now the day of their wedding had arrived. Gazing out of the window at the sparkling sunshine, Harper tried to swallow down the nerves inside her. These were not the normal jitters a bride might feel on her big day, those of anticipation and excitement. No, Harper's nerves were of the more sinister kind, sitting like a leaden weight in her stomach.

Never had she imagined her wedding day would be like this—that she would be facing it so completely alone, without even Leah by her side. Vieri had offered to pay her flight, insisting that her being here wouldn't be a problem for him, that whatever had gone on between them was all in the past. But Harper had declined. She had no intention of even telling Leah that she was marrying Vieri. What was the point? It wasn't real. In a few months the marriage would be annulled and it would be as if it had never happened. And besides, if she told Leah it would be all round Glenruie before you could say capercaillie. Leah couldn't keep a secret to save her life.

Taking her dress from the wardrobe, Harper unzipped it from its garment bag and laid it over her arm. It was made of fine cream silk, with a loose cowl neck and a low back. This was the first time she had actually held it in her hands, and she was taken aback by just how lovely it was.

She had bought it online, having no intention of going to any of the bridal boutiques in Palermo and running into another of Vieri's admirers. Instead she had chosen it from the vast array of wedding dresses available, rapidly scrolling through them, refusing to spend too much time deliberating over the seductive creations because what did it matter what she looked like anyway? It wasn't as if she had a lover waiting for her at the altar, desperate to see his beautiful bride. Vieri would probably barely even notice what she was wearing.

Taking off her robe, she slipped the dress over her head. It slithered down over her body, pooling in a perfect circle at her feet. It was almost laughable the way it was such a perfect fit, as if it had been made for her. The slippery silk encased her slender body, showcasing her bare arms, her décolletage, the gentle swell of her hips, her long legs. Allowing herself only the briefest of glances in the mirror, she sat herself down at the dressing table and set about taming her curls into some sort of order, sweeping them up into a loose chignon. She would do this, she would put on some make-up, then she would make her way to the chapel and she would marry Vieri Romano. What she wouldn't do was think. Because thinking about what she was doing had the capacity to break her heart.

'This is all very sudden, *mio amico*.'

Vieri glanced across at his oldest friend. He and Jaco had been raised together in the children's home but, unlike him, Jaco had been adopted at the age of eleven and whisked away to a shiny new life. At the time they had pretty much lost touch, but years later, when Jaco was living in New York, they had renewed their acquaintance. By then they were both highly successful businessmen and both enjoying the playboy lifestyle. Standing well over six feet tall but having lost none of his boyish charm, Jaco had rivalled Vieri for the affections of the city's most beautiful women, or so he liked to keep telling him. But there was no doubting that the two of them had been a formidable force when they had hit the town together.

'Well, you know how it is, Jac.' Deliberately vague, Vieri shifted his weight from one leg to the other, checking his watch again.

The two men were standing beside the altar of the chapel, waiting for the bride to appear. The small congregation was chattering amongst themselves, the priest bending down to talk to Alfonso, who had had his wheelchair positioned right at the front so that he would miss nothing.

'I'm not sure I do.' Jaco gave his friend a sideways glance. 'I thought we had both agreed that the whole marriage thing wasn't for us.'

'Well, yes.' Vieri tugged at the sleeve of his shirt. 'But things change, don't they?'

'And would this sudden change be anything to do with your godfather?' Jaco narrowed his eyes. 'I understand he doesn't have a lot longer on this earth.'

'I want to make him happy, Jac. It's the least I can do.'

'Even so, getting married... Isn't that a bit extreme?'

Vieri shrugged and Jaco followed his gaze in the direction of Alfonso, who looked up and gave them a beaming smile.

'There's your answer.' Vieri returned his eyes

to the front. 'That look has got to be worth a bit of self-sacrifice.'

'If you say so, old friend.' Jaco patted Vieri on the shoulder. 'If you say so.'

With a low rumble and a couple of hollow squeaks, the organ music started up and the congregation fell silent. Moving into position in front of the altar, Vieri stood tall and straight, pushing back his shoulders, gazing up at the arched stained-glass window. As the slightly wheezy strains of Vivaldi's Primavera filled the intimate but echoing space he found himself saying a silent prayer, asking for guidance, or absolution, or at least some sort of indication that he really was doing the right thing. For suddenly this wedding felt terrifyingly real.

A sharp dig in the ribs from his friend interrupted his thoughts. 'Self-sacrifice, eh?' With a low laugh, Jaco, who had been looking over his shoulder, returned to face the front. 'I'm not sure that's what I'd call it. She's a stunner Vieri.'

But Vieri had no time to reply. With a swish of silk Harper had come to stand beside him and finally he turned to look at her, only for the breath to be sucked from his lungs. Because she looked exquisite. The simple dress sheathed her gentle curves and slithered to the floor. She carried a small bouquet of white gardenia, with a single bloom tucked into her hair behind one ear, and as he stared at her a shaft of coloured light flickered over her face and down her body, giving her an ethereal, almost other-worldly appearance.

Vieri forced himself to drag in some air. He had never expected this, to have such a visceral reaction to his bride, so strong that it threatened to undo him completely. He told himself that it had to be guilt, for what he was making her do, what he was putting her through. But the way his mind was already slipping the silky garment down her body, his fingers itching to explore the exposed skin beneath, had nothing to do with guilt. Neither did the inexplicable surge of emotion that had suddenly consumed him, coming out of nowhere, so strong that it burned behind his eyes, held his muscles taut. It was a wave of tenderness, of possessiveness. The feeling, no, the certainty that Harper would be his and his alone. From this day forth.

They held each other's gaze and for a split second Vieri saw all the torment and confusion he was experiencing reflected in Harper's remarkable hazel eyes. *And the desire.* Yes, she felt it too, no matter how much she might try and deny it. That, at least, gave salve to his masculine pride.

The priest gave a small cough, opening the heavy bible in his hands, preparing to start the ceremony. But he had barely uttered more than a few words from the opening address before

the door at the rear of the chapel squeaked open,
then closed again, followed by footsteps hastening
down the aisle that defied all but the most stoic
not to turn and see who this latecomer might be.

'Sorry, sorry.' There was no mistaking that accent or who it belonged to as the apologies continued and the guests shuffled along to make room
for her at the end of a pew.

'Leah!' Harper had turned to look at her sister, whispering her name in astonishment before
frantically mouthing, What are you doing here?

Seated now, Leah gave her an apologetic grin,
followed by a little wave, which turned into a dismissive gesture to get on with it.

Harper turned back to the front. 'Your doing,
I take it?' she whispered under her breath, her
eyes fixed straight ahead, but there was a smile
in her voice.

Vieri shrugged in admission. It was true he had
ignored Harper's instructions not to invite her sister, going behind her back and sending Leah the
money for her flight here. He wasn't even sure
why he'd done it, except that he had strongly felt
that it was time Harper's family supported her,
instead of it always being the other way round. It
was time they realised just how lucky they were
to have her.

When Leah hadn't shown this morning he had
written her off, assumed she had just taken the

money, ripped him off again. But it seemed he had been wrong.

'There are *two* of them?' To his right he heard Jaco utter his astonishment but Vieri wasn't going to start explaining now. He would, however, put his friend right about that young woman the first chance he got. If ever anyone had trouble written through them like a stick of rock, she did.

As Harper took her seat at the head of the table she hardly recognised the ancient dining room that had been transformed for the wedding breakfast. The draughty, echoing room had had a serious makeover: colourful antique rugs covered the cold flagstone floor, red velvet chairs replaced the uncomfortable carved wooden ones, and the table had been beautifully laid with a white damask tablecloth set with silver gilt cutlery and sparkling crystal. Arrangements of winter flowers, interspersed with cream candles in gilt candlesticks, ran the length of the table. In fact there were candles everywhere, positioned on the polished wood furniture at the sides of the room and in the heavy iron candelabra above their heads. A roaring fire blazed in the enormous grate.

'The wedding planners have done a good job.' Vieri eased himself into the seat beside her. 'I'll have to remember to use them again.'

'For your next wedding, do you mean?' Avoiding his eyes, Harper smiled sweetly at the assembled guests as she shook out her napkin and placed it on her lap.

'I actually meant commercially—my hotels host a lot of weddings.' Vieri gave her a dark stare. 'I have no intention of marrying again.'

'Oh, my mistake.' Accepting a glass of wine from the waiter, Harper let her shoulders drop from where they had been hovering up around her ears. They were married now, deed was done, there was no point in being all prickly with Vieri. That would solve nothing. She might just as well relax and enjoy the meal as best she could.

She cast her eyes down the long table. Leah was sitting about halfway down, next to Vieri's friend, Jaco. Harper had to admit it was lovely to have her here, and secretly she was touched that Vieri had gone to the trouble of arranging it. She couldn't hear what they were saying but under Jaco's instruction Leah was swilling the wine around in her glass, then holding it to her nose to inhale the bouquet. Jaco was laughing.

At the far end of the table, Alfonso was holding court with a couple of elderly friends. Feeling Harper's eyes on him, he looked up and smiled, raising his glass.

'Look at him.' Vieri leant in closer and immediately Harper's senses leapt about in response. 'I can't remember the last time I saw him so happy.'

Raising his own glass in return, he waited for Harper to do the same. 'We did the right thing, you know.'

Harper nodded. For the first time this whole crazy venture made sense. For the first time she could see why they had done it. To give pleasure to a kind and generous man who deserved happiness at the very end of his life. For the first time it felt as if they had done something good.

'Yes, we did, didn't we?' She turned and smiled at Vieri, clinking her glass against his, and as their eyes met Harper felt her stomach somersault inside her.

'I'm glad you agree.' Holding her gaze, Vieri studied her face intently before covering her hand with his own. 'You have a lovely smile, by the way. You should use it more often.'

Harper quickly looked away, battling against the crippling effect of the unexpected compliment. Gripping the stem of her glass, she took a sip of the velvety wine. If her smile was lovely, his was deadly, used for the sole purpose of killing his prey.

She had been fighting his devastating attraction all day, since the moment she had come to stand beside him in the chapel. Dressed in an immaculate grey suit, with matching waistcoat, and a blue silk tie that mirrored his ultramarine eyes, Vieri was the embodiment of sheer masculine perfection. His dark hair was pushed back from his forehead, curling behind his ears. When he was clean-shaven, his thick sideburns appeared more obvious, as did his square jaw and that oh-so-sensuous pink mouth. A mouth that brought back the memory of how it had felt against her own. That begged to be felt there again.

Setting down her glass, Harper took a shaky breath. Today, more than any day, she needed to be careful. She had to be on her guard, protect herself from the deadly onslaught of Vieri's charm. And step one was to try and steady the traitorous thump of her heart right now.

In true Sicilian style, the meal went on for hours. Course after course of delicious food was served, accompanied by freely flowing wine that ensured all the guests had a good time. Day soon turned to night, and as the more elderly guests started to leave Alfonso eventually announced that he was going to retire. Calling Vieri and Harper over, he embraced them warmly as they bent to kiss his cheek, taking hold of Harper's hand as she straightened up and patting it affectionately.

'Thank you so much, both of you. This has been wonderful.' He smiled up at them but as the smile faded a seriousness crept into his eyes. 'I hope you know how much it means to me.'

'We do, *padrino*.' Vieri squeezed his shoulder. 'And we are very glad that you have enjoyed the day.'

'I don't just mean the day.' A hint of impatience crept in as Alfonso gripped Harper's hand with surprising force. 'I'm talking about the two of you being officially married.' He paused and Harper could see just how tired he was. 'I must admit, I had my doubts. You might even call them suspicions.' His bushy eyebrows lowered over eyes that flicked between Harper and Vieri. 'In fact I did wonder at first if the two of you had cooked this up between you. A well-intentioned but misguided plan to fool an old man.' Harper froze, her gaze locked on Alfonso's hand so that she wouldn't have to meet Vieri's eye.

'But then I saw the two of you together and my mind was put at rest. Because I could see it in your eyes, feel it here, in my heart.' He banged his chest with his fist. 'I could see that you loved each other. And that was all that mattered. Which was why I hurried things along a bit.' He gave a low chuckle.

'You mean it wasn't because you are dying!' With a leap of hope, Harper blurted out the words.

'Oh, bless you, my dear. I'm dying all right.' Alfonso kissed her hand. 'But now, I can die in peace, safe in the knowledge that my godson has finally found the happiness he deserves.'

Harper forced down the lump in her throat, fighting the tears that pricked the backs of her eyes.

'Anyway, enough of my old-man ramblings. I hope that you young people will continue to celebrate long into the night. Oh, I nearly forgot.' Reaching into his inside jacket pocket, he withdrew an envelope and passed it to Vieri. 'A wedding present. Open it later.'

'Thank you, *padrino*.' Vieri put the envelope into his pocket. 'You are very kind.'

'And you are very dear to me, both of you, I want you to know that. Come, one last embrace.' Holding out his arms, he pulled them down into a long hug before kissing them in turn on the cheek. 'Now it is time to say goodbye.' His voice wavered. *'Addio, miei cari!'*

He signalled to Maria, who had returned to the *castello* just in time for the wedding. Taking hold of the handles of his wheelchair, she waited for Alfonso to release the brake before slowly wheeling him out of the room. As Harper and Vieri watched him go, he raised a shaky hand of farewell above his head.

CHAPTER TEN

'WELL, GOODNIGHT, YOU TWO.'

Always the last to leave a party, Leah finally got to her feet and moved unsteadily around the debris-strewn table. She kissed Harper, and then, rather more awkwardly, Vieri.

'Thank you so much for inviting me, Vieri, and for paying for my flight and everything so I could be here. That was very generous of you. Especially after what I did…letting you down like that.'

'Forget it.' Vieri waved his hand in a dismissive gesture but Harper noticed there was no rancour in his voice. He looked and sounded positively mellow.

'And can I just say…?' She paused, a smile spreading across her face. 'You two make a lovely couple.'

'Leah!' Harper shot her sister a warning glare.

This was typical of Leah, stirring things up. They had had very little time to talk but during

a hushed conversation in the privacy of the bathroom Harper had made sure that her sister knew
the score, that this was a marriage in name only.
Except, of course, Leah refused to believe it.

'I can't help it if that's what I think.' Leah refused to be silenced. 'And I'm not the only one.
Everyone has been saying so all day.'

Had they? Even though Harper knew that
that was just what people said at weddings, she
couldn't help but feel a little surge of pleasure. Because somehow, despite everything, even though
it shouldn't have, today had been lovely. It had
felt right.

She put it down to the fact that she and Vieri
had achieved their aim—they had made Alfonso
happy. In fact, he had appeared positively delighted, a beaming smile across his face for most
of the day. Which in turn had made Vieri relax.
Harper had seen a new side to him as he had
chatted to the guests, laughed with Jaco, clearly
enjoying himself. Even now, at this late hour, he
appeared to be in no hurry to end the day; instead
he cradled a glass of brandy in his hand, absently
swilling the liquid around as he watched the sis-
terly exchange going on. If Harper wasn't mistaken, there was the tug of a smile pulling at the
corners of his mouth.

'Go to bed, Leah.' Sitting up straighter, Harper
shooed Leah away. 'I'll see you in the morning.'

'I'm going, I'm going.' Blowing them both a kiss, Leah tottered off, her feet bare, her strappy shoes held over her shoulder by one finger. 'Have a good night, you two.'

Alone at last, a dangerous silence settled over the room. Harper cleared her throat.

'Well, I guess I had better be thinking about going to bed too.'

'Yes, it's been a long day.'

'A successful one though.' She looked across at Vieri for confirmation but immediately found herself caught in the midnight blue of his eyes. Pulling her gaze away, she only made it as far as the long length of his body lounging back in his chair. With one leg crossed over the other, he appeared completely at ease and even more dangerously handsome than ever. The jacket had gone, the fitted waistcoat emphasising his broad shoulders, his narrow waist. He had loosened his tie and pushed up the sleeves of his shirt to reveal tanned forearms, covered in a liberal dusting of dark hair. He looked casual, relaxed, but most of all deeply, heart-wrenchingly sexy. Harper felt her chest tighten.

'No regrets, then?' Lightly asked, his question nevertheless demanded an answer.

'No. I'm glad that we were able to do this for Alfonso.'

'Good.' He took a sip of brandy. 'That makes me feel less guilty.'

'Guilty?' Harper laughed. 'I can't imagine you ever feeling guilty about anything.'

'Then that shows how little you know me.' Suddenly serious, Vieri leant forward in his chair.

Harper blinked. 'That's true.' She really did know very little about this enigmatic man who was now, remarkably, *ridiculously*, her husband.

'Then perhaps we should do something about it.'

'Like what?' Her words came out as a gasp.

Vieri shrugged his elegant shoulders. 'I would be lying if I didn't admit that a few things were coming to mind.'

Their gazes clashed, the *few things* he was referring to all too clear in the swirling depths of his eyes. Harper felt the frantic beat of her heart in her throat.

'You are a very special person, Harper.' The sincerity of his gaze held her captive. 'I really mean that.'

'Well, thank you.' Harper gave an embarrassed laugh but it was silenced by a fingertip pressed against her lips.

'And I would very much like to make love to you.'

Shock ricocheted through her, swiftly followed by a clench of lust, deep in her groin. It was the way he had just *said* it, as if it were so easily possible, as if it could just happen. Which of course it could. Harper swallowed hard. But it *shouldn't*, should it?

Fighting to find some logic, some reason in this swirl of madness, Harper stood up, gazing at the vaulted ceiling as if the answer had to be hiding there somewhere. 'But this was never part of our agreement.' Her voice sounded husky, as if it belonged to someone else.

'Hang the agreement.' Suddenly up on his feet, Vieri came and stood before her, cupping her chin in his hand. His cool façade had slipped, revealing the dark passion beneath. 'Right now I want you, Harper. You have no idea how much.' His breath feathered across her heated face, his words sending spasms of yearning right through her. 'And I believe you want me too.'

'Yes.' Harper stared into his eyes, suddenly unable to hide the truth any longer.

A smile curved Vieri's sensuous mouth. '*Bene.* So what do you say? Will you let me take you to bed tonight?'

Oh, God. Harper had never wanted anything more in her life. But she couldn't just say yes. Could she?

'I… I don't know, Vieri.' Still she tried to rationalise her thoughts that now only drummed with one, sensuous beat.

Reaching forward, Vieri picked up a stray tendril of hair and, after a moment's hesitation, tucked it behind her ear. 'One night together, Harper, that's all I'm asking, all I'm offering. One night of pleasure.'

It was so tempting. He was so, so tempting.

'I think we deserve that.'

Did they? Harper had no idea what they deserved. But as Vieri's face came towards her she felt her eyelids flutter closed and when his lips touched hers she knew she was powerless to resist. The kiss deepened immediately, the tidal wave of sensation kicking in again until the pleasure was so strong she couldn't feel her feet any more, didn't know which way up she was. With his lips moulded against her own, firm and tight, yet silky and persuasive, their hot possession left no room for doubt or thought of any kind, and she could do nothing but let herself be pulled into the swirling abyss, dragged under by the current, left gasping for air. It was suffocating. It was drowning. And it was impossible to fight.

She wanted him! And even though a quiet voice told her to be careful, warned her of the consequences, a much louder one was screaming at her to do this. To let go, to live for the moment. That if she didn't, she would regret it. The sort of regret that would stay with her for the rest of her life.

Breaking away from the kiss, she felt for his hand, tipping her head to look up at him, still needing that final confirmation. And there it was.

With his pupils dilated until his eyes were almost black, Harper had her proof. She could see that he was hanging onto the very last threads of his control and that was all she needed to know. He wanted her every bit as much as she wanted him. And that was the most empowering feeling ever.

'Let's go.' With a confidence that surprised her, she tugged on his hand, leading him out of the dining room. But by the time they had reached the echoing hallway, Vieri was beside her, one arm around her waist, hurrying them both up the long flight of stairs as if the very devil were on their heels. They flew down the corridor together until they reached their bedroom door.

Or at least the bedroom that they supposedly shared. In fact, as far as Harper knew, Vieri had never so much as set foot in there. True to his word, from day one he had found himself another room in the *castello*, Harper didn't know where. She had told herself she didn't care. So she alone had used this bedroom, slept in the ornate 'marriage' bed, dressed in front of the fancy gilt mirror. And even though she had told herself it was a relief, that the last thing she had wanted was the awkwardness of sharing a room with Vieri and all the mixed emotions that would have stirred up, in truth it had only made her feel more alone.

But tonight all that was going to change. Opening the door, Vieri pulled her in behind him but the sight that met Harper's eyes stopped her in her tracks. The bedroom had been filled with candles, burning low now that several hours had passed. In the flickering light, Harper could see a trail of rose petals leading to the bed, the four posts of which had been decorated with winter foliage and long-stemmed red roses, twisting up and around and over the canopy, giving it a wonderful, Sleeping-Beauty-like quality.

'It seems the wedding planners have been busy.' She gave a light laugh, intended to show that she knew this ridiculously romantic setting had no real heart behind it, had nothing to do with Vieri.

'So it would seem.' He looked around him, puzzled.

'I think we can probably guess whose idea this was.' She raised her eyebrows, giving Vieri a neutral smile.

'Alfonso!' They spoke his name together.

With a low laugh Vieri took hold of her hand and navigated them along the path of petals towards the bed. 'He is completely shameless. He will stop at nothing to bring us together.'

'I know.' They sat down together on the bed, Harper's heart banging loud enough to wake the entire *castello* as she looked at their hands clasped together in Vieri's lap, thought of where they might soon travel. 'And it seems he has succeeded.'

'Yes.' The air between them thickened, vibrating with desire. With his fingers stroking against her palm, Harper felt her eyelids close, her whole body tingle with erotic awareness.

'You want this?' His breath whispered softly against her face.

'I want this, Vieri.'

She had never wanted anything so much in her entire life. It was an all-consuming yearning that obliterated all doubt, took all reason and turned it into so much dust. The need for him to be hers, to possess her, as no man ever had, was so strong, so overwhelming, that it didn't matter that she knew they had no future together. Tomorrow didn't matter. *Hell*, an hour's time didn't matter. All that mattered was that Vieri took her in his arms and made love to her right now.

Opening her eyes, she gazed at the chiselled features of his handsome face, registering the slash of heat beneath the olive skin, the determined set of his jaw showing his restraint, the way he was holding back. But most of all she saw the swirling depths of desire in his eyes; she saw how much he wanted her. And that was all she needed.

Her hands flew to his chest, rapidly unbuttoning his waistcoat and pushing it over his shoulders before pulling his tie undone. She moved to start on the buttons of his shirt but Vieri took over, sweeping her effortlessly from the bed and setting her onto the floor where his hot gaze swept over her, scorching her flesh from head to toe. Kicking off her shoes, Harper stood on tiptoe to reach for him, linking her arms behind his head, suddenly aware of the difference in their heights, how very tall he was. But feeling for her hands, Vieri released their grasp and took her arms above her head, so that her breasts tugged upwards. Their eyes met.

'Stay like that.' It was a hoarse demand, a whisper of promise.

Bending down, he took hold of the hem of her dress, bunching the slippery fabric in his hands and starting to lift it up, revealing her ankles, then her calves. As he rose to standing he took the dress with him until it had slithered past her bottom and her waist and, with a final flourish, like a triumphant matador, he pulled it up and over her head.

'Molto bella.' Tossing the dress to one side, Vieri took a moment to look at her, his eyes travelling hungrily over the white silk stockings, the matching panties, and then to her breasts, naked and heavy with need. But Harper felt no shyness as his gaze raked over her, no embarrassment or awkwardness. Instead his intense gaze empowered her, made her feel beautiful, as if she could do anything. She tingled with a glorious heat that

spread to every cell in her body, finding its way to her core where it burned hot and bright and insistent.

Only when his eyes alighted on the scar that arced down one side of her belly did she falter, her arm instinctively moving to cover it. But Vieri lifted her hand, running his finger tenderly along the fine ridge of the scar tissue.

'What's this?'

'A kidney transplant. Years ago, when I was sixteen.' She spoke quickly, hoping that would be explanation enough.

'You needed a kidney transplant?'

'No, not me, Leah. I was the donor.'

'*Cristo*, Harper.' Vieri moved his hands to her shoulders, bringing her closer to him. 'Has your entire life been dedicated to saving others?'

'Pretty much.' Harper pulled back to look into his eyes.

'And now?'

'Not now. Trust me, Vieri, this…' She moved provocatively against him. 'This is just for me.'

'For us.'

'Yes,' she corrected herself. 'For us.'

With a slow, sinful smile, Vieri reached to release the pins in her hair and Harper shook her head so that the loose curls tumbled over her shoulders, over her naked breasts.

'You look…' he swallowed hard '…incredible.'

His words brought a heady surge of power, stripping away any last inhibitions, making her bold, making her sure. Never had anyone looked at her like that before, made her feel like this before.

Her hands moved back to his shirt again, fumbling with the buttons until she was able to push the fabric apart, expose Vieri's broad, muscled chest to her greedy eyes, her itching fingers. She placed the flat of her palms against the wall of his chest, revelling in the feel of his hot, hard skin, the brush of tight, coarse hair. His muscles flexed beneath her touch, his obvious strength and power thrilling her senses, tightening her core still further. She closed her eyes, letting herself feel the beat of his heart, picking up the rhythm with her own pulse that pumped the blood rapidly through her veins.

Vieri moved to shrug off his shirt, then dealt with the buttons of his fly, pulling off his trousers, along with his shoes and socks. Down to black boxers now, straining against the power of his arousal, he stood gazing at her for a couple of long seconds, silent apart from the telling rasp of his breath. Then, dispensing with his last item of clothing, he waited, watching her watching him. Harper's eyes widened. With his naked body illuminated by the candlelight he looked like the embodiment of perfection in masculine form. So virile, so potent, so totally magnificent.

He reached for her again, sweeping aside the curtain of her hair and leaning forward to breathe against her neck, then plant a trail of hot, heavy kisses from below her earlobe to the base of her throat.

Trembling with anticipation, Harper felt his hands slide down her arms, over her waist, to the top of her thighs above her stockings where his fingers sensuously traced the bare flesh, circling inwards towards her very centre. Harper gasped, his velvet touch stealing her breath, clenching every muscle in her body, turning her inside out.

Her small step closed the space between them, trapping his hands where she wanted to feel them so very badly, at the very heart of her, the heat of her, her most sensitive core. But Vieri took his hands away, pressing them firmly against her buttocks, clenching hard to pull her against him so that the gloriously, shocking swell of his arousal pressed against her tummy. Harper drew in a sharp breath of shock.

'For you, Harper,' he moaned softly before covering her mouth with his own, kissing her tenderly, but with such possession, such need, that there was no doubting his intent. 'Just wait one second.'

Pulling away, he crossed over to where his trousers had been discarded on the floor and, slipping his hand into the pocket, he brought out a foil wrapper. Ripping it open with his teeth, he turned to face her again, sliding the condom over his magnificent form with practised ease.

Then he was hers again, spanning her hips with his hands and lifting her effortlessly off her feet. Harper threaded her arms around his neck, Vieri's soft Sicilian curse sounding like the most erotic word in the world as he moved them backwards onto the bed where he laid her down, his body held over her by locked elbows on either side of her head.

He kissed her again, his hand moving between them to trace the flimsy silk of her panties, before removing them to brush against her tight curls as his fingers found their way to her centre that throbbed, hot and wet and desperate with need. Harper squirmed into his touch, silently urging him on until one finger unerringly found just the right spot and he started a torturous, teasing, circular movement. With a wild gasp, she grasped at his shoulders to anchor him down, to give her more. He expertly increased the pressure until Harper felt herself start to shake, a tremor spreading through her body, taking her over completely. With a sigh she gave herself over to it, closing her eyes and drifting with it, shuddering more dramatically with each wave that rippled through her, dimly aware, but not caring in the least, that her small mews were growing louder with each blissful, clenching contraction.

Eventually she stilled as Vieri's hand withdrew. She opened her eyes.

'Sie bellissima!'

His lips closed over her mouth again as he re-positioned himself until he was exactly where he wanted to be and with a deep, shuddering thrust, accompanied by a groan of pleasure, he was inside her.

She gasped out loud, the sharp twinge of pain holding her rigid, clawing her nails into his back.

'Harper?' Immediately he stopped, pushing himself up on forearms ridged with corded veins as he stared down into her face.

'It's nothing.' Harper made herself breathe and the pain was gone, replaced by the most glorious sensation of fullness, of being joined, as she felt her tightness expand to hold him. She put her arms around his neck to pull him back down. 'Really.'

'Harper, if you want me to stop…'

'No!' That was the very last thing she wanted. She raised her head to find his lips, digging her hands into his hair. And after a moment of hesitation he was kissing her back, lowering his body, sliding further into her with slick, juddering sureness that felt more right than anything she had ever felt before.

He started to move, slowly at first, but increasing the speed with the rasp of his breath, his thrusts becoming deeper, faster, until Harper felt the dark waves of ecstasy start to roll again and, with a glorious sense of abandonment, she gave herself over to this most incredible of sensations. She heard Vieri groan, utter something low and primal in his native tongue as with one, last punishing thrust he shuddered his own release, deep inside her, before falling down to be wrapped in her arms.

CHAPTER ELEVEN

VIERI STIRRED, OPENING his eyes to see a shaft of moonlight illuminating the bed. He looked down to where Harper was asleep in his arms, her face buried in his chest so that all he could see was the tangle of auburn curls. His heart swelled. She looked completely adorable.

A strange feeling of pride came over him, a sense of peace. Closing his eyes again, he listened to her soft, even breathing, inhaling her unique scent, so different from his own, mixed in with the smell of flowers and candle wax in the room.

He had never expected to find himself here. At the start of yesterday he had been thinking about nothing other than getting the wedding ceremony over with, getting the day over with. He had been totally convinced that this was to be a union in name only, and a very temporary one at that. But as the day had worn on, something had shifted inside him.

Spending time with Harper, watching her talking to the guests, to Alfonso, always with that quiet charm, that easy grace, had made him realise just how exceptional she was. He had found his eyes following her around the room, seeking her out, an unfamiliar sense of pleasure stealing over him when she returned to his side. Jaco had soon picked up on the vibe, ribbing his old friend about *getting a room*, steadfastly refusing to accept Vieri's account that this marriage was simply a means to an end. In fact it had been Jaco who had slipped the condom into his pocket, giving him a hug and muttering 'just in case' in his ear before retiring to bed.

And, of course, Jaco was right. What Vieri felt for Harper went way beyond an appreciation of her social skills, or her ability to make his godfather happy. The idea that that was all it was was laughable. The simmering attraction between them had been there right from the start but slowly it had become more than that. It had become something bigger, more whole, affecting him on a deeper level altogether. He had refused to face up to it. Until tonight.

Tonight he could ignore his feelings no longer. Tonight he had been able to think of nothing else but taking her in his arms and making love to her. The attraction between them, both physical and mental, had become an all-consuming need that he had been powerless to resist. Suddenly he'd found himself asking why not? They were consenting adults. They were actually married, for God's sake. What was to stop them enjoying one night together? And once that idea had taken hold, nothing was going to budge it.

And the reality had been better than even his overheated imagination could have come up with. Sex with Harper had been amazing. *Special.* Maybe too special. Vieri realised that for the first time ever the sexual act had actually meant something, gone far beyond simple physical pleasure and taken him somewhere he had never been before, deep into unknown realms of emotions that he hadn't even known existed. It felt dangerously like losing control, but for this one night he was going to allow himself to live solely in the moment, enjoy the here and now. He wasn't going to think, he wasn't going to analyse what had happened between them, or indeed the fact that Harper had clearly been a virgin. Not now. Not with her nuzzled like this in his arms. He felt himself drifting off into a contented sleep but when Harper moved softly against him, his arousal, which had already half woken from its slumber, defiantly made itself known.

'Vieri.' His name, uttered sleepily from her open lips, only served to stoke the fire, and when she reached for him, pressing her full breasts up against him, winding her legs around his, there was only one possible outcome. One hot and sensual, deeply sexual and infinitely satisfying conclusion.

Harper awoke with a start. The room was very still. A watery, early morning daylight was filtering through the gaps in the old wooden shutters. Pulling the covers under her chin, she stared at the foliage twisted around the posts of the bed, the roses that had lost their just-picked bloom.

She was alone. She knew that much without turning to look or spreading out a limb to check. She could sense the space where Vieri had been, feel it with a twitch of pain, like a hole in a tooth.

He had gone. Screwing her eyes shut, she forced herself to get a grip, to ignore the clenching of her heart, the acute sense of loss, abandonment.

She had known the deal when she had agreed to go to bed with Vieri. *One night of pleasure.* That was what they had signed up for. And clearly that night was over.

She turned on her side, staring at the indentation on the pillow where Vieri's head had been. Despite the sense of emptiness inside her, she didn't regret what they had done—she could never regret it. Because making love with Vieri had been the most wonderful experience of her life. She had felt it; it had happened. She was irrevocably changed. And even though the bed beside her was empty now, nothing could take that away.

Pulling back the covers, she caught sight of the crumpled pair of white stockings, remembering how Vieri had peeled them from her legs, some time in the middle of the night. How they had made love again, with such passion, such tenderness...but without a condom. She recalled Vieri cursing with frustration, searching his pockets again, coming back to bed empty-handed. But the power of their passion had been too strong and neither of them had had the willpower to stop. Instead Vieri had insisted that he would be very careful. She just hoped he was right.

Picking up the stockings, she rolled them into a ball and tossed them onto a chair before heading for the bathroom and a long, hot shower.

She sensed something had happened the moment she stepped out into the corridor. At first all seemed eerily quiet, but as she strained her ears she could hear low male voices and as she started to descend the sweeping staircase the two men in the hall looked up at her. Friends of Alfonso's, they had stayed overnight. Harper started to smile at them but her smile froze as she got closer and caught the sombre expressions on their faces.

'My dear.' One of them reached out and touched her arm. 'I am so sorry.'

Panic clawed at her heart. 'W…what?'

'You…you haven't heard?' The two men exchanged a glance.

'No, tell me, please. What has happened?'

Just then the door to the study opened and Vieri appeared, his face ashen grey.

'Vieri!' Harper rushed towards him but he seemed to look straight through her.

A man in a dark suit followed him out and together they walked to the front door, speaking in soft but rapid Sicilian. Harper watched in frantic silence as they shook hands, the man pulling Vieri into a hug, patting him on the back, before turning to leave.

'Vieri! Please, tell me what has happened!' She ran to him again, putting her hands on his chest to bar his way, to prevent him from walking straight past her.

Vieri stopped, looking at her for the first time, and Harper felt her heart contract with pain. His handsome face was taut with grief, his eyes the colour of dull stone. He dragged in a breath, as if having to speak to her was costing him too much, more than he was prepared to give. But eventually he found the coldly terse words.

'It's Alfonso, Harper.' He averted his gaze, as if he couldn't bear to look at her. 'He's dead.'

'No!' Harper choked on the word, tears immediately brimming in her eyes. 'But how…when?'

'Some time last night.'

'Oh, Vieri.' Harper stared back at him, tears starting to roll down her cheeks. He took several steps away from her, then stood tall and straight, as imposing as ever, but with every plane of his body rigid with tension. As if, were she to touch him, he might snap. 'I'm so sorry.'

He angled his head, giving an almost imperceptible shrug, as if to say her platitudes were of no interest to him. As if she were of no interest to him. This man, who only a few hours ago had looked at her as if she was the centre of his world, taking her to unknown heights of ecstasy, *stealing her heart*, was now regarding her with something bordering on disgust.

But he was grieving. Taking a shuddering breath, Harper wiped the tears from her cheeks with the back of her hand. He looked so devastated, so lost, that she thought her heart might break for him.

Her feet took her towards him again, the overwhelming need to comfort him blocking out all other emotions. Throwing her arms around his waist, she tried to hug him to her, but it was like hugging a block of stone. And when she crushed her head against his chest, her tears dampening the front of his shirt, it seemed as if his heart beating against her ear had slowed to a cold, hard thud.

He made an impatient noise over the top of her head. 'I need to get on. There are a lot of things I have to see to.'

'Yes, of course.' Harper sniffed noisily, pulling herself away. She cleared her throat, tucking her hair behind her ears. 'Can you just tell me...was anyone with him when he died?'

'Maria was with him.' His voice was dry, detached. 'She said it was very peaceful.'

'Well, that's something to be thankful for.' Harper sniffed again. She waited for some sort of reply but his silence made it all too clear that she was being dismissed. 'Okay, I'll...um...let you get on, then.' She started to move away. 'But if there's anything I can do to help, anything at all, you will say, won't you?'

'Actually there is.' The force of his reply turned her hopefully back to face him.

'Yes?'

'Get rid of the guests.' His mouth flattened into a hard line. 'All of them. Right away.'

Harper hesitated, but only for a second. 'Yes, of course.'

She hated the thought of having to tell people that Alfonso had died but if it saved Vieri the painful chore then she would do it.

'And that includes your sister.' He fixed her with a cold stare, devoid of all emotion.

'Very well.' With a sombre nod, Harper moved

away. She would do as she was told. Now was definitely not the time to question his orders.

'Entra.' Vieri briskly replied to the tap on the office door. Pinching the bridge of his nose, he tried to stem the headache that was building behind his eyes. He had been dealing with all the paperwork involved with Alfonso's death for a couple of hours now, and, even though he was grateful to have something to keep his mind occupied, he knew he needed a break. He sat back in his chair waiting to see who the visitor was, inexplicably finding himself hoping it was Harper. He had been unnecessarily brusque with her—she was probably owed an apology.

But it wasn't Harper. And as the door opened the sight of who it actually was saw Vieri leap to his feet.

'You!' Anger surged through him, hot and fierce. 'What the hell are you doing here?'

'Well, that's not much of a welcome, I must say.' Advancing into the room, Donatella moved around the desk to stand beside him. 'You seem to have forgotten your manners, Vieri.'

She was wearing a fur coat and had some sort of small dog tucked under her arm, who stared at Vieri with bulging eyes.

'I have forgotten nothing, trust me. And you are not welcome here.'

'Now, don't be like that.' She tried to offer her cheek to be kissed but Vieri jerked his head away, stepping to the side. The thought of kissing this woman made him want to be sick.

'I mean it, Donatella.' Her name tasted like poison on his tongue. 'I want you to leave.'

Totally ignoring him, Donatella moved to seat herself in the chair opposite the desk, settling the dog on her lap. 'Surely you will allow me to pay my respects.'

'*Respects?*' Vieri spat the word back at her, his body rigid with tension. 'I think it's a little late for that. I don't recall you showing Alfonso any respect when he was alive.'

'As I recall, *he* disowned *me*.' She stroked the dog's fur with a hand heavy with jewelled rings. 'And me his only living relative.'

'And you know full well why. You made your lethal choice when you married into the Sorrentino family.'

'Ah, yes, of course. I am the evil witch responsible for the extermination of the Calleroni family.'

'For the murder of your father, Alfonso's only brother, yes.'

'Look at you, Vieri, so high and mighty, so morally upright.' A sneer curled her lip. 'And yet I seem to recall a time when even knowing who I was, *what* I was, didn't stop you from coming to my bed.'

Vieri ground down hard on his jaw, not trusting himself to speak.

'You were crazy for me once, Vieri. You can't deny that.'

'I was crazy, all right, crazy to ever have anything to do with you.'

'Ah, I see the years have twisted the truth, *il mio amore*, made you bitter. But I'm sure you must remember the good times. I know I do.'

'What I remember—' Vieri sucked in a breath '—is that you made the decision to terminate our unborn child!'

Shock flickered across Donatella's face, fighting to move the chemically frozen muscles. 'So you know about that?'

A murderous silence filled the air. 'I do.'

'Then you should be grateful.' Swiftly recovering her composure, Donatella lifted her chin.

'Grateful?' The word roared between them.

'Yes, grateful that I swiftly dealt with the situation. Surely you didn't think you and I would ever be playing happy families?'

'Maybe not.' Fury slowed his words to a low drawl. 'But that doesn't mean I couldn't have raised the child myself. Had I ever been consulted, that is.'

'Trust me.' She gave a harsh laugh. 'No amount of *consultation* would have persuaded me to keep that baby.'

Rage flowed thickly through Vieri's veins like molten lava. He towered over her, his fists clenching and unclenching as he fought to find some control. 'Leave! Now!'

'Very well, I will go.' Rising to her feet, Donatella tucked the dog under her arm and started towards the door, but then stopped, turning to look at him again. 'Oh, how rude of me. I haven't congratulated you on your marriage.' She met his searing glare. 'Such a charming young girl, that little wife of yours. Did she tell you we had met?'

Pure hatred whitened the skin around Vieri's mouth.

'Yes, of course she did. I'm sure you two don't have any secrets.' She gave him a sly smile. 'No doubt she will be only too happy to bless you with any number of little brats if that's what you want. I wish you a long and fertile life together.'

Vieri's low growl gave him away and Donatella's gaze sharpened.

'Or have I got that wrong? Perhaps there is another reason for this hasty marriage?' She raised a painted talon to her lip, pretending to think. The dog squirmed in her grasp. 'Could it be something to do with your godfather's imminent demise, I wonder? Something in the terms of his will that meant if you weren't married, his money, this *castello*, would have come to me?'

'Ha!' Vieri laughed in her face. How typical of Donatella to assume that she was the reason for his rushed marriage. 'Trust me, that was never going to happen.'

'That's just it, I don't trust you, Vieri.' She stared at him with calculating eyes. 'I have watched your meteoric rise to fame, seen the way you have acquired exposed businesses, taken over failing companies. That takes ruthlessness, determination, grit. Qualities I like to think, in some small way, you may have learnt from me.' She studied her fingernails.

'Or to put it another way, I believe that over the years you have become every bit as manipulative and underhanded as me. I believe you will stop at nothing to get what you want, especially if that means depriving me of any inheritance. I just hope that poor unsuspecting young woman you have taken as your bride knows what she's let herself in for. For her sake, I hope she knows the man you really are.'

'Get out!' Vieri roared with a violence that made the dog growl, bare its teeth. Marching past her, he flung open the door, standing sentry as she came towards him.

'Don't worry, I'm going. *Ciao, mio caro.*' She reached up to touch his cheek but Vieri ducked away from her hand. 'Until we meet again.'

Ushering her out into the hallway, Vieri turned

and strode back into the office, slamming the door behind him.

One thing was for sure: if he had any say in it, they would never, *ever*, meet again.

Harper heard the slam of the door before she turned the stairs and saw Donatella Sorrentino standing outside the office. She stopped, her hand gripping the banister, a cold fear creeping up her spine. There was something about this woman and her relationship with Vieri that felt bad, dangerous. Harper had never forgotten the way Vieri had reacted when she had told him about Donatella choosing her dress. It had been extreme, violent even. And now this, the door slamming, the high colour of Donatella's cheeks as she headed for the front door, proof positive that emotions between her and Vieri were running high. Harper didn't know what those emotions were but she did know that they were deeply felt and still very much alive. Which logically only led her to the conclusion she had already suspected. At some point in time, Vieri and Donatella had been lovers. And they possibly still were.

Pushing that hideously painful thought to the back of her mind, she watched as Donatella reached the front door, desperate for the woman to be gone. But at the last minute Donatella turned, fixing Harper with an icy stare, and for a moment their eyes locked.

'Good luck.' Donatella broke the heavy silence with a caw of sarcasm. 'You are going to need it.' Then with a cruel laugh she turned and swept through the front door.

Harper sucked in a breath. She refused to be intimidated by her, refused to even think about who this woman was, what part she played in Vieri's life. Not today, not on the day of Alfonso's death.

Moving to stand outside the office, she was trying to pull her composure into place when the door flew open and she was suddenly confronted with Vieri's towering figure. And judging by the murderous look in his eye, a towering mood to match.

Harper's heart lurched with love and compassion and a myriad other emotions that she couldn't begin to process right now.

'Hi.' She sounded ridiculously chirpy. 'I was just coming to tell you that I've done as you asked. All the visitors have left or are leaving. They asked me to pass on their condolences, and Jaco said to tell you he will be in touch later today.'

'Fine, whatever.' With a shrug, Vieri looked over her shoulder, scanning the empty hallway.

'If you are looking for Donatella, she has just left.' Harper fought to keep the bitterness, any sign that she cared, out of her voice.

'But you are still here.' The dark blue eyes swung back in her direction, coldly focussing on her face.

'Well, yes, of course.'

'There's no of course about it. I want you to leave too.'

'Me?' Harper stared at him in astonishment.

'Yes, you.' He squared his shoulders, determination setting in. 'I want you to go. I don't want anybody here.'

'But I'm not "anybody", Vieri.' Harper gasped. 'I'm your…' She hesitated, the word *wife* refusing to come. Despite what had happened last night she was not his wife, not in the true sense of the word. And she never would be. 'I loved Alfonso, you know I did.'

'You barely knew him.'

'Not like you, no, but that doesn't mean I'm not deeply saddened by his death, that I'm not grieving too.'

'Well, you can go and grieve somewhere else.'

'Vieri!' Horror stiffened her spine. That he could be so hurtful, so cruel, cut her to the quick. But he was in shock. Dragging in a stuttering breath, she forced herself to calm down. 'Look, you're upset. I'm sure you don't mean that.'

'I can assure you, I do.'

She stared back at him, the glimpse of his vulnerability beneath his granite façade the only thing keeping her strong. 'Let's not discuss this now. We can talk things over later.'

'There is nothing to talk about, Harper.'

'Don't do this, Vieri. Don't push me away. I want to be here for you, to be able to support you.'

'The way you *support* everybody else, I suppose?'

Harper flinched at the bite of his words. 'What do you mean by that?'

'I mean that I don't need your support, Harper. More than that, I don't want it. You don't need to fix me, the way you seem to have to fix everyone else in your life.'

'That's not fair, Vieri.'

'No? Well, that's the way it looks to me. It strikes me that you are so busy solving everyone else's problems that you have never stopped to take a long hard look at your own. Not content with saving your sister's life, it seems you have to carry on running it for her. And the same with your father, trying to control everything he does.' He paused, his eyes glittering like flint. 'Perhaps if you spent a bit less time meddling in other people's lives and a bit more concentrating on your own you wouldn't still be a virgin at the age of twenty-five.'

Harper gasped, her eyes widening in horror. It took a second or two for his vicious words to permeate, for it to sink in that he had really said them. But when it did her knees started to tremble beneath her and she had to reach for the wall to support herself. The blood drained from her face, taking her breath along with it, so that she had to fight to remain upright. She swallowed, made herself breathe, then swallowed again.

She could feel his eyes on her but she would not look at him. There were a thousand things she wanted to say but none of them would come. And none of them mattered, anyway. All the words in the world wouldn't have made any difference. With his short, brutal analysis Vieri had made it quite clear what he thought of her. He had shown just what a sad, pathetic creature he considered her to be. And maybe he was right. Maybe she had spent all her life looking out for other people because she had no life of her own. Maybe to still be a virgin at the age of twenty-five was pathetic. Pitiful. And if that wasn't, finally giving her virginity away to a man such as Vieri Romano certainly was.

But worse than that, far far worse, was the fact that her virginity wasn't the only thing she had given him. She had given him her heart. And for that she would never forgive herself.

Moving away, she headed blindly for the stairs, tightly gripping hold of the banister to help in her ascent, all too aware of Vieri's cold, cruel eyes trained on her every step. She forced her shoulders back and straightened her spine, determined at least to hang onto her last modicum of pride while she still had it. Because right now, it felt as if that was all she had left.

CHAPTER TWELVE

VIERI WATCHED AS Harper climbed the stairs, her chin up, her head held high. But he could see just how much effort it was costing her, just how much his spiteful words had hurt her. He cursed violently under his breath, only just stopping himself from screaming out loud. Why the hell had he done that? Taunting her about her virginity, of all things. Why had he taken out his fury and hatred for Donatella on Harper? It was unforgivable.

But deep down he knew why. *Guilt.*

Much as he hated to admit it, Donatella had been right when she had called him manipulative and underhand. That was the man he had become. Hadn't he demonstrated both of those qualities in the way he had treated Harper, using her purely for his own gain? *His own pleasure.* She had been right too, when she'd said he had learnt from her, but not in the way she'd meant. His poisoned relationship with Donatella had taught him never to trust anyone, never to get close to anyone. Never to give his heart away again. Something he had to guard against now, in a way he never had before.

He jammed his hands deep into his pockets, pacing to and fro across the echoing hallway.

Discovering that Harper had been a virgin had shocked him to the core. He had taken something from her that she would never get back. Something that he most certainly didn't deserve. Now the shame of his action refused to go away. So when Harper had looked at him with those wide hazel eyes, piercing his protective armour, his guilt had made him lash out.

But maybe she had brought it upon herself. Vieri allowed his twisted logic to kick in. Maybe it was her fault for insisting on searching for the goodness in him, looking for something that wasn't there. Didn't she realise there was no goodness to be had? For all his wealth and success, all his urbane charm and effortless good looks, he was nothing more than a fraud. An empty vessel, a hollow shell. The baby his parents hadn't wanted, the boy no one had adopted, the misguided young lover who had been rejected, the father he was never allowed to be. He certainly didn't deserve her kindness and compassion. Much less her virginity. *Or her love.* If he allowed her to get close to him now he would only end up dragging her down, ruining her life, and he would never let that happen. He had to set her free.

Turning to go back into the office, he blinked against the tortured image of her face as he had delivered his spiteful words—the shock, hurt and pain, that awful pain that had stolen the light from her eyes.

He had to be strong. Alfonso was dead; there was no longer any reason for them to be together. It was better to be cruel now and have a clean break than prolong this agony any longer.

His phone buzzed in his pocket and he viciously swiped to accept the call from the funeral directors. *'Si, pronto.'* Kicking the office door shut with his foot, he spoke in rapid Sicilian, instructing them to come and collect Alfonso's body as soon as possible. No, he did not want them to leave his godfather at the *castello* for a period of mourning. He had no intention of prolonging this particular agony either. As painful as it was, he would say his goodbyes now, and that would be an end to it.

Standing outside Alfonso's bedroom door, Vieri steeled himself for what was on the other side. Slowly turning the handle, he let himself in. The large, panelled room was dimly lit and a chilly breeze stirred the air. The shutters were closed against the bright daylight outside but one window was open behind them so that, in accordance with Sicilian tradition, the deceased soul could fly off to heaven.

As his eyes adjusted, Vieri could make out the motionless shape in the bed. Alfonso, his dear *padrino*, really was dead. The harsh reality slammed into him again. He silently stepped forward and only then did he realise that there was someone else in the room. Harper. Sitting quietly by the bedside, her head bowed, her hand clasping one of Alfonso's that lay stiffly outside the covers. But the second she saw Vieri she was on her feet.

'Oh, it's you,' she whispered hoarsely. 'I'll go.'

'You don't have to.' His voice sounded gruff, unsteady.

'Yes, yes, I must.' She refused to look at him. 'You will want to pay your respects in private.'

He moved to stand beside her, inexorably drawn to her the way he always was. The masochist in him made him want to see her face and he reached to take hold of her chin, lifting it so that she had no alternative but to meet his stare. But what he saw shrivelled his very soul. Her eyes were red from crying, long eyelashes clumped together, the tears still damp on her cheeks. She looked so unutterably sad he simply couldn't bear it.

'What I said earlier, Harper.' All his resolve

had vanished at the sight of her misery and he slipped an arm around her shoulder to pull her against him. 'I'm sorry.'

'Not here, Vieri.' She put a shaky hand to his chest, lightly pushing him away. Vieri could feel the heat from her palm warming his heart. 'This is not the time or the place.'

'No.' Letting his arm drop, Vieri glanced down at his godfather. 'Of course not.'

For a moment she held his gaze, her eyes dark, unfathomable. Then, blinking, she turned away, bending to plant a soft kiss on Alfonso's forehead.

'I'm going now, Vieri.' Straightening up, she tossed her hair over her shoulders, tucking it behind her ears, suddenly in control. But Vieri saw the pale column of her throat work with the effort of swallowing. 'I have never seen the point of long goodbyes.'

'No. I understand.' He moved to let her pass. 'The undertakers will be here soon anyway.'

Giving him one last heart-rending look, Harper brushed past him and left the room.

Vieri took the seat where she had been and picked up the hand that she had been holding. Old and gnarled, it felt cold to his touch. He raised it to his lips, letting his breath warm it, just for a minute, before replacing it carefully down on the coverlet. He gazed at his godfather's face, so familiar, so much loved, and yet somehow already different. As if he was no longer there. As if his soul had already left his body.

He would miss him so much, this man who had always been there for him, guided his path in life, steered him in the right direction, stopped him from making the worst mistake of his life. They had never discussed the whole Donatella debacle. Not once. Because that wasn't Alfonso's way. He knew how stubborn Vieri was, how proud. Instead he had cleverly manipulated him away from trouble, given him the means to start a whole new life.

With a flash of long-overdue insight, Vieri realised that Alfonso had been manipulating him right up to the end. His marriage to Harper. He raised his eyes heavenward. Was it possible that the wise old goat had been right about that too? Certainly everything about last night had felt right, more than right. Amidst the shock and grief of Alfonso's passing it didn't seem appropriate to let his mind go there but if he did... then he knew that his body still thrummed with the high of it, yearned for more. He knew that no other sexual experience had come close, that making love to Harper had been on another level completely. It had touched him. It had *meant* something.

I have never seen the point of long goodbyes.

Suddenly Harper's words came back to him and he knew, with a bone-chilling certainty, that she hadn't just been talking about saying goodbye to Alfonso. She had been saying goodbye to him.

He jumped to his feet, his heart racing in his chest, his first instinct to run and find her, to stop her, to beg her forgiveness. *To ask her to stay.* But dredging up a depth of willpower he scarcely knew he possessed, he forced himself to stop. He would not go after her. For her sake he *had* to let her go.

There was a light knock on the door and Agnese, Alfonso's housekeeper, appeared in the doorway. 'Signore Romano, I thought you should know that the funeral directors are here.'

'*Si, grazie.*' With a heart laden with sadness, Vieri bent over his godfather to place one last kiss on his cheek. Then, straightening up, he took a deep breath and nodded. 'Tell them I will be right there.'

The sun shone brightly on a thin scattering of snow that coated the rugged landscape as Harper neared her home on the Craigmore estate. Ahead of her Mount Craigmore, one of the Scottish Munros so beloved by serious climbers, stood tall and proud, its jagged white peak stark against the blue sky.

It felt strange to be back, even though she'd

only been away for a few weeks. Everything looked the same, but felt different, as if there had been some imperceptible change. With a twist of sadness Harper realised that she was the one who had changed. Irrevocably and for ever.

Leaving Sicily, leaving Vieri, had all but torn her apart. But she had done it, somehow made the arrangements, taking the first flight she could from Palermo, and spending half the night at Amsterdam airport waiting for a connection rather than spending another moment on Sicilian soil.

And despite the fact that she felt as if she had been passed through a grater, mercilessly shredded, a quick glance down revealed that she was still in one piece. Still breathing. Nobody died of a broken heart. She would get over this, be strong, carry on. Because that was who she was, what she did.

The first test of her strength had been telling Leah, who had been sleeping soundly through the drama going on around her at Castello di Trevente. Harper had already woken her to tell her the news of Alfonso's death and the fact that Vieri wanted her to leave. But Leah was still in bed when Harper returned with the knowledge that she too would be going.

'Hurry up, Leah.' She pulled impatiently at the bedclothes. 'I've already told you, we have to leave.'

'*We?*' Pushing herself up onto one arm, Leah had stared incredulously at her sister. 'Surely you're not leaving too?'

'Yes. I told you, Vieri wants everyone to go.'

'But not you, surely?' She frowned deeply. 'I mean, you and Vieri, yesterday, you seemed so close.'

'It was an act, Leah. You of all people should know that.' In the effort to cover up her pain and hurt she knew she sounded harsh, cold. But it was either that or break down and burst into tears and she would fight against that with all her will. Because if Leah knew that Vieri had broken her heart she wouldn't put it past her to insist on confronting him, to rush to take a chunk out of him there and then.

'Well, if it was an act, it was a very good one.' Leah gave her sister a narrow-eyed look. 'It certainly had me fooled.'

'But that's not exactly difficult, is it, Leah?' Harper snapped back. 'I seem to remember you getting fooled by a certain Max Rodriguez and losing all that money being the reason we are in this mess right now. Or should I say *I* am in this mess.'

'And you know how sorry I am about that, sis.' Leah reached for Harper's hand, her eyes imploring.

'I know. I'm sorry, Lea, I don't mean to keep

punishing you.' Harper dragged in a breath, fighting to keep the emotion at bay, acutely aware that Leah was watching her intently. 'It's just…it's all been a bit much. What with the wedding and everything and now Alfonso dying.'

'Of course.' Leah pulled an apologetic face. 'I'm sorry about Alfonso, really I am. He seemed like a lovely man and I know how fond you were of him. But…' her face brightened '…it does mean that your ordeal is over now.' She paused, searching Harper's face. 'Doesn't it?'

If only. If pretending to be Vieri's fiancée, and then his wife, had been the ordeal, then what she felt now, the thought of being separated from him for ever, was more akin to torture. She swallowed down her misery and focussed on the practicalities.

'It would be if we didn't happen to be legally married.'

'Well, presumably that can be annulled or something, can't it?' Leah persisted, her eyes not leaving her sister's face. But when Harper didn't immediately reply she leaned in closer. 'Harper?'

'I don't know…yes… I suppose so.' Even amongst all the trauma of the day that particular worm of worry had managed to niggle at the back of her brain. She and Vieri had consummated the marriage, more than once. Did that mean it could no longer be annulled? But right now that problem would have to wait. Right now, all she could think about was getting away.

She had assumed that she and Leah would travel back to Glenruie together, but Leah, being Leah, had had other ideas.

'So are you planning on staying at Glenruie, when we get back?' She asked the question casually as she moved around the room collecting her belongings.

'Yes, of course. What else would I do?'

'Only I was just wondering, if you are there to keep an eye on Dad, could I maybe be excused, just for a week or so? It's not like he needs both of us on his case.'

'And what would you be doing for this *week or so*?' Harper helped her close her suitcase.

'Well, the thing is—' Leah affected a nonchalant air '—Jaco, he's invited me to go to Licata to see his vineyard.'

'Has he now?'

'And obviously I said no, because I thought I had to get back to Glenruie.'

'Obviously.'

'But now…'

Harper shook her head, even managing a small smile. She had never been able to deny her sister anything. And there was no reason why one of them shouldn't be happy. Jaco had seemed like a nice guy, and as Vieri's oldest friend he had to be trustworthy, didn't he?

'I mean, I will come back with you now if you want me to, that goes without saying.'

'No, it's fine!' She took Leah's hand. She had to admit that a part of her was glad that Leah wouldn't be accompanying her back home. She wasn't sure her fragile armour would be able to withstand several hours of Leah's questioning. At least this way she would be able to nurse her misery in peace. 'But promise me you won't do anything stupid.'

'Who, me?' Leah had feigned an innocent look, before pulling her sister into a hug.

So Harper had travelled alone. Now, as she paid the taxi, picked up her bag and trudged across the crunchy grass to let herself into Gamekeeper's Cottage, wondering what havoc would greet her inside, she felt more desperately miserable than at any time in her life.

Vieri hastily gathered together his belongings, the urge to get away from the *castello*, from Sicily, suddenly overwhelming. He would fly back to New York right away, concentrate on getting his life back on track. A life that had recently become dangerously derailed.

Today he had buried his godfather. In the same chapel that he had married Harper only forty-eight hours before, he had had to endure the ceremony, then watch as Alfonso's body was lowered into the ground. And as the priest had given his final blessing and Vieri had scattered a handful of soil against the polished wood, he had never felt more alone.

But he only had himself to blame. Because there was only one person who could have made this day more bearable. *Harper.* And he had driven her away, banished her. Today he had missed her presence like a physical pain but the suffering was no more than he deserved. Much as he had longed for the feel of her hand in his, for the comfort and support she could have given him, he had had no right to it. Far from it.

And the brutal fact was, even with the funeral over, he still missed her. With Harper gone it felt as if a huge void had opened up. As if a part of him had died.

And this was he, Vieri Romano, a man who prided himself on needing no one. Who had learned from a very young age to stand on his own two feet, to fight his own battles. To look to no one for emotional support, or any other support come to that. Even his beloved *padrino* had had to use his cunning and intelligence to circumnavigate Vieri's fierce pride before he could offer any guidance or advice.

Moving over to the wardrobe, he started to

roughly pull his shirts off the hangers. He had ordered Harper to leave the *castello* and she had done just that, even though missing Alfonso's funeral must have hurt her terribly. He had behaved like a heartless bastard—he knew that. But he also knew that he was doing this for her own good, to save her from himself. Because the longer she was around him, the more deeply they became involved, the worse it would be for her in the long run. He would end up destroying her. And he couldn't bear for that to happen.

Plucking his wedding suit from the hanger, Vieri started to shove it into his suitcase when he felt the rustle of something in the jacket pocket. Sliding his hand in, he pulled out an envelope. Alfonso's wedding gift. Caught up in the events of his wedding night he had completely forgotten about it. Now he sat down on the edge of the bed and withdrew the handwritten piece of paper. He read it quickly, his godfather's reassuring voice speaking the words in his head.

To my dearest Vieri and Harper,
It is my final wish that you accept Castello di Trevente as my wedding gift to you. I know it was agreed, Vieri, that my entire estate would be distributed amongst my charities, but I hope you will allow me this small change of heart.

The thought of the two of you living here, raising a family, gives me the greatest of pleasure. I know you would never deny me that.
Your loving godfather,
Alfonso.

Vieri put his head in his hands, screwing up his eyes against the shame and guilt. Alfonso's gift, so generously given, so optimistically stated, felt like a ton of salt poured onto an open wound. Because he and Harper would never be living together at Castello di Trevente, let alone raising a family here. The whole thing had been a big fat lie. And Alfonso's kindness had only exposed the nasty little fraud for what it really was.

Getting to his feet, he raked a hand through his hair, then turned and stuffed Alfonso's letter into his suitcase, slamming down the lid. He would tell Harper about the 'wedding present' at a later date, when he had calmed down. She could have the whole *castello* as far as he was concerned, to live in or to sell, or to give to her wretched sister if that was what she wanted. It didn't matter to him. All that mattered was getting away from here.

Picking up his suitcase, he cast one last look around him and then headed out of the door. He couldn't get back to New York fast enough—back to the ordered, controlled life he had had before this whole wretched debacle had kicked off. Before Harper had happened. Only then would he be able to think straight again.

CHAPTER THIRTEEN

HARPER STARED AT the tester stick held in her shaky hand. *No.* She screwed up her eyes, refusing to believe it. It wasn't possible; it couldn't be true. But when she opened them again, they were still there, the two bright pink lines. There was no doubt about it—she was pregnant.

She let a couple of seconds pass, waiting for the reality to sink in. *Pregnant.* The room did a giddy spin. Whatever was she going to do? However was she going to cope?

Grasping hold of the washbasin beside her, she pulled herself to standing and faced herself in the mirror. She was pregnant with Vieri Romano's baby. And she had absolutely no idea what to do about it.

'Harps, hurry up, I need the loo. Whatever are you doing in there?' The bathroom door rattled and the old bolt that had never been very secure obligingly slid open. Spinning round, Harper saw

Leah standing in the doorway. 'Oh, God, sis, you look dreadful. Are you ill?'

'No, no, I'm fine.'

'Well, you don't look fine. Whatever's the matter?'

'Nothing, I told you. Can't I even get five minutes' peace in this house?'

Leah advanced into the room. 'What are you hiding behind your back?'

'Nothing.'

'Oh, Harper!'

'What?' In her befuddled state Harper had failed to realise that the tester stick, still clasped in her hand behind her back, was reflected in the mirror.

'You're not!'

Letting out a long, juddering breath, Harper nodded miserably.

'Oh, my God!'

Flinging her arms around her sister, Leah hugged her tightly, then pulled away so she could see her face. 'It's Vieri's?'

Harper nodded again. She didn't have the strength to ask who the hell else's it was likely to be.

'But you said…'

'I know, Lea. It was just that one night, the night of the wedding.'

'Golly.'

'Yes, golly.' Somehow the use of the old-fashioned and ridiculously understated word broke the tension and suddenly the two sisters started to laugh, clinging to each other for all they were worth.

'So, what are you going to do?' Finally breaking away, Leah studied Harper's semi-hysterical and now tear-stained face.

'I… I don't know.' She accepted the bunch of tissue that Leah had plucked from the toilet roll and blew her nose. 'I mean, obviously I'm going to keep it. And I'll have to tell Vieri at some point. But not yet. Not until I've got used to the idea.'

'Don't leave it too long.' Leah dabbed at her sister's eyes. 'It will only make it harder in the long run.'

'I guess so.' A sudden panicky thought occurred to her. 'But whatever you do, don't you go telling him, Leah! You must promise me that.'

'Yes, of course, I promise. I wouldn't do that. What do you take me for?'

Harper shot her a look, which Leah studiously ignored.

'Oh, sis, this is so exciting! I'm going to be an auntie.' She clasped Harper's hands in hers, which only set Harper's lip trembling more violently.

Exciting was one word for it—petrifying another one. However was she going to get through this? Not just with the pregnancy or the birth or the prospect of raising a child on her own. But the fact that this was Vieri's child.

She had worked so hard to try and forget about him, done everything she could to block him from her thoughts, erase him from her mind. But of course it had been impossible. Six weeks had passed since she'd left Sicily, six torturous, lonely weeks when there had been no contact between them at all. And far from finding any relief, each week had felt more bleak, more desolate than the one before. Despite Harper keeping herself frantically busy, watching her father like a hawk, overseeing his job as well as working shifts at Craigmore Lodge, Vieri still managed to consume her every waking moment. More than that, he had tortured her dreams, images of the night they had spent together filling her head, crowding her sleep until she woke to the gnawing agony of being alone again.

And now this. A baby. A living, breathing child that would tie them together for ever. Somehow she was going to have to protect her shattered heart from the onslaught of having Vieri in her life. Because he would insist on being there for his son or daughter; instinctively Harper knew that. Supposing he tried to take the baby away from her? Supposing he decided to fight her for custody?

'Don't look so worried!' At the sight of her troubled face, Leah pulled her into a hug again. 'Everything will be all right. We'll do this together. I'll be there every step of the way.'

Harper gave a weak smile, surrendering to her sister's embrace. Somehow that statement did absolutely nothing to reassure her.

Getting out of the car he'd hired at the airport, Vieri slammed the door and looked around him. This place was picturesque, he'd give them that, but right now picturesque didn't cut it. Right now he just wanted to reach his destination. It felt as if this journey to Glenruie had gone on for ever— first the flight from New York to Glasgow and then following the seemingly endless road along the side of a glittering loch. And now the sat nav had brought him to some ancient-looking contraption that called itself a car ferry, and, even though he had been ready to leave as soon as he'd bumped the car up onto it, it seemed that the two men in the tugboat that pulled the thing across the inlet were going nowhere. He marched over towards them.

'Can we get a move on, please?' He tapped his watch for emphasis. They looked back at him with mild lack of interest. 'I'm in a hurry.'

'We're a waitin' more vehicles.' The older one spoke through the window of the tug in a language that Vieri only barely recognised as English.

More vehicles? They could be here all night. Apart from the odd battered old Land Rover he hadn't seen a car for twenty minutes. Vieri scowled.

'Where ya headed, any road?'

'Glenruie.'

'Craigmore Lodge?'

'Yes, well, the Craigmore estate.' Vieri hesitated, having no desire to discuss the reason for his visit with these two. But if it meant getting there more quickly... 'I'm looking for the gamekeeper's cottage. I have business with Harper McDonald.'

'Do you now?'

Irritation spiked inside him. Hadn't he just said that?

'Yes. So, could we get going?' Vieri attempted to keep his impatience in check.

'Aye, why not?' With an incomprehensible but immensely welcome change of heart, the old man started the engine of the tugboat. 'Close the gates, Jim. We cannae keep this man away from Miss McDonald any longer. He looks like he's fair set to bust.'

Turning on his heel, Vieri went back to sit in his car, drumming his fingers on the steering wheel as the ferry chugged its way across the inlet of blue water that was supposedly quicker than driving around this peninsula. He wasn't entirely sure what *set fair to bust* meant, but he could hazard a guess. Clearly he wasn't managing to hide his feelings anything like as effectively as he'd thought.

His decision to come to Scotland had been made on the spur of the moment. He'd been in a board meeting at his New York office, staring out at the city skyline when he should have been concentrating on the latest capital investment accounts, when the idea had come into his head. Picking up the phone, he had instructed his jet to be put on standby, telling his driver to take him to the airport there and then, before logic and common sense had the chance to change his mind. As the board members had been hastily shepherded out of the room they had exchanged nervous glances. What was Romano playing at? What the hell had come over him these past few weeks?

The fact was, Vieri didn't know what had come over him. Only that he had been back in New York for two months now and that time had done absolutely nothing to erase Harper from his mind. Being halfway across the other side of the world had done nothing to free him from the power of her spell. Even throwing himself into work, where he normally felt his most comfortable, had failed spectacularly. Instead of finding any relief there he had ended up making questionable judgements, bad decisions.

Which meant only one thing—he had to see Harper. As soon as possible. Right away. He was done trying to forget about her; he was sick of hearing his own damned voice telling him that he had to get over her. This was the only way.

As the ferry finally docked on the other side Vieri started the car engine, gritting his teeth at the casual way Jim was sauntering over to open the gates. Now that he was so close he could almost sense Harper's presence, almost feel her in his arms.

Mio Dio, how he had missed her. From the toss of that auburn-coloured hair, to the pout of her pink lips, the way she wrinkled her nose when she was annoyed, bit down on her lip as she thought. Her bright intelligence, her sexy body, her slow smile, he missed them all. With a passion that was burning him up inside.

One thing was for sure, if he didn't get off this ferry and reach his destination very soon, there was a good chance that he might indeed be *fair set to bust*.

Harper eased herself up against the pillows, checking how she was feeling. The cramps had definitely stopped. It had to be, what, at least a couple of hours now since the last one? She allowed herself a sigh of relief, the hope in her chest starting to bloom. Maybe, just maybe, it was going to be all right.

The first muscle spasm had woken her early that morning. Low in her abdomen, it hadn't been painful, but enough to see her fumbling for the bedside light and lying very, very still. Then the second one had come, followed by a third until a cold rush of fear had swept over her that something was wrong. Levering herself gently out of bed, she had stood in the cold first light, hoping against hope that being upright might help, that each spasm might be the last, but still they had come.

Clutching her stomach, she had tried to swallow down the panic. It was only two weeks since she had done the pregnancy test but already the thought of losing this baby was too terrible to contemplate. Already she knew that the child inside her was more important, more precious than anything in the world. No matter what obstacles lay ahead, no matter that being tied to Vieri would break her heart a thousand times, she would fight with everything she had to keep it safe. Starting now.

Pulling on her clothes, she had crept downstairs, trying not to wake Leah, surprised to find her already in the kitchen, nursing a mug of tea.

Apparently she had got up to make their father his breakfast and seen him off to work. And of course one look at Harper's face had been enough for her to know that something was wrong. Refusing to take no for an answer, she had leapt into action, bundling her into the Land Rover and delivering her to the local doctors' surgery just as they were opening their doors.

And the doctor had been reassuring. After taking down the details, her professionalism slipping only very slightly at the news that Harper McDonald, who she had known since she was a baby, was pregnant by some unknown man, she had given her a quick check over and made an appointment for her to have an ultrasound scan.

'And try not to worry.' She had patted Harper's hand, now devoid of both the engagement ring and the wedding band that Harper had tugged off her finger and hurled onto the dresser before fleeing from the *castello*. 'It's early days and we can't completely rule out that there may be a problem but sometimes these cramps are just the baby bedding in. I suggest you go home and have twenty-four hours of bed rest. Let your sister look after you.'

Bedding in. It had been such a cosy, comforting expression. Leah, who had insisted on coming in with her, had turned to give her a smile full of hope, reassuring the doctor that she would wait on Harper hand and foot for the whole nine months if necessary.

Which was why Harper now found herself in the unfamiliar position of lying in bed with absolutely nothing to do. And that meant too much thinking and all thoughts inevitably led to Vieri. She rearranged the pillows and sat back, staring out of the window at the dark shape of the mountains against the thundery grey sky. *She was in love with him.* It was as simple and as complicated as that. And there was absolutely nothing she could do about it. But he still didn't even know she was pregnant. Closing her eyes, she let herself drift off to sleep, promising that she would find the courage to tell him as soon as she knew for sure that everything was all right.

Vieri pulled the car up in front of the cottage. So this was where Harper lived. It was smaller than he'd imagined; a long, low, white building with dormer windows set into a slate roof. But he could see the logic in building low to the ground in this rugged landscape. It was beautiful but it was also tough and wild, the climate unpredictable. Attributes that might describe Harper herself.

Pulling up the collar of his cashmere coat against the fat drops of rain that were starting to fall, he rapped hard on the knocker of the weather-beaten door. His heart, he suddenly re-alised, was beating over-fast. From inside he heard a dog bark and a female voice telling him to shush. There was a rustle as she came closer, the skittering sound of the dog's claws against a hard floor. Vieri took in a breath, pulled back his shoulders.

But it wasn't Harper. As the door opened, Leah appeared, holding the straining dog by its collar. She stared at him in open-mouthed shock.

'What are you doing here?' Her question was straight to the point, but Vieri could hear the panic in her voice.

'I have come to see Harper.'

'Well, I'm sorry, it's not convenient.' She made an attempt to bar the door.

'Then I will wait until it is.' Firmly planting his feet and towering over her, Vieri made it quite clear that he was going nowhere.

'Look, the thing is…' Leah went for a different approach. 'Harper's in bed. She's not well.'

'What sort of not well?' A thrum of alarm moved through him and he took a step forward, leaving Leah no option but to move aside to let him in. Ignoring the growl of the dog, he ducked his head and stepped inside until the three of them were squashed in the small hallway. Leah squeezed past him, dragging the dog behind her. Vieri followed them into the kitchen, where the dog was finally persuaded to go and lie down in his basket next to the Aga. Leah turned to face him.

'Can I get you a drink of anything?' Vieri could see her struggling to hold her composure. 'Tea or coffee, I mean—we don't have alcohol in the house.'

'No, nothing.' The more he looked at Leah, the more convinced he was that there was something seriously wrong. 'Tell me now, Leah, what's the matter with Harper? Is she ill?'

'Umm, not…not really.' Leah turned to fill the kettle but Vieri was behind her in a couple of strides, his hand on her shoulder, turning her to face him.

'And what exactly does that mean?'

'It means that she's not ill in the conventional use of the word.'

'For God's sake, Leah.' Irritation and alarm thrummed through him. 'I refuse to stand here listening to your riddles. Either you tell me what is wrong with your sister right now, or I climb those stairs and find out for myself.'

'No!' Leah clutched at his elbow. 'Don't do that. She needs quiet. She mustn't have any stress.'

'Then tell me what's going on.'

'I can't!' Shrugging from under his grip, Leah moved into the room, backing towards the wall.

'Harper made me promise I wouldn't say anything to you.'

'About what?' The blood was beginning to roar in his ears. 'You have precisely three seconds, Leah.'

'About the baby!' She blurted out the words with a cry of anguish. 'Oh, God…' She looked at him with beseeching eyes. 'Harper is going to kill me.'

But Vieri wasn't listening any more. The roaring in his ears had intensified to the point where he couldn't hear anything anyway. A red mist had descended, clenching his fists, making his whole body tremble with a flood of thundering rage that had all but engulfed him.

The baby. Leah's words ricocheted inside his head. So Harper *was* pregnant? Or at least she *had been* pregnant. He screwed his eyes closed against the violent realisation that the deed must have already been done. Why else would Harper be in bed? Why else would Leah look so damned shifty? *Guilty.*

A thousand splintered thoughts shattered in his brain. When had it happened? If he had got here yesterday could he have stopped it? Or even earlier today, if the journey hadn't taken so long, if that infernal ferry hadn't been so slow? Why had he let his pride keep him away for so long? Why had he ever let Harper out of his sight?

But most of all was the hideous sense of history repeating itself. He had done it again. Let down his guard, let someone in. First Donatella and then Harper. And once again he had been betrayed.

Anger surged inside him, hot and febrile. He forced himself to drag in a breath, dimly aware that Leah was speaking. No doubt she was complicit in this; she had probably arranged the whole thing. Vieri couldn't bring himself to look at her. She was irrelevant. But Harper…*oh, Dio*… His beautiful, seductive, tormenting Harper. Was it possible that she could really have done this? He lifted his head, squaring his shoulders. There was only one way to find out.

He moved through the kitchen, Leah leaping ahead of him, trying to bar his way, holding her hands up against his chest.

'No, Vieri, you mustn't go up there.'

'Get out of my way, Leah.'

'No, really, the doctor said she needed rest.'

'I said get out of my way.'

The dog had joined in now, growling loudly. Stepping past them both, Vieri headed for the stairs, Leah following him before turning to shut the dog in the kitchen.

'Please, Vieri, I'm begging you.' She called up from the bottom of the stairs. 'Don't go upsetting her. I know I shouldn't have told you but now it's done…'

Now it's done. With his thumb on the iron latch of a bedroom door, Vieri turned to look down at Harper's twin. So there was his proof. Giving Leah one last glance of utter revulsion, he clicked the latch down.

CHAPTER FOURTEEN

THE LOUD RAP on the front door, followed by
Timmy's barking, woke Harper from her doze.
She heard Leah going to answer the door, but
the next sound froze her with shock. A male
voice, deep and impatient. *Vieri!* No, it couldn't
be. Clutching at the bedclothes, she told herself she must have made a mistake. Her sleep-
fuddled state, her anxiety over the pregnancy,
had obviously conjured him up from the shad-
owy recesses of her mind, where she had tried
so hard to banish him. But then she had heard it
again, his voice raised now as they went into the
kitchen. There was no mistake. Vieri was here,
in this house, under this roof.

Oh, God. Harper tried to rationalise her
thoughts over the frantic thudding of her heart.
*What was he doing here? And why did it suddenly
feel as if all the oxygen had been sucked from the
room?* She forced herself to calm down, for the
sake of the baby, if nothing else. But still her mind

madly darted in all directions as she tried to figure out how she was going to face him, what she
was going to say. She just hoped Leah would be
able to distract him long enough for her to pull
her defences in place.

I am pregnant, Vieri, she tried the words in
her head. *But I intend to raise the child myself.*
No, that sounded too contentious. *I feel that any
decisions regarding the child's future should be
left to me.* As if he would accept that. But before her poor frazzled brain could come up with
anything remotely workable she heard the com-
motion going on downstairs. Timmy was growling, Leah pleading and Vieri… He sounded so
angry. So filled with rage. A rage that was coming closer and closer with his every thunderous
step. And then, with a click of metal and a creak
of the hinges, the door flew open.

Vieri stared at her. Propped up in bed by pillows,
she was clutching the duvet under her chin, as if
it could somehow protect her. Well, there was no
chance of that. There was nothing in the world
that would be able to protect her from the storm
that raged inside him now.

He advanced towards her, trying to ignore the
way his heart flipped at the sight of her, the fact
that, somewhere at the calm centre of that storm,
the sight of her was still managing to affect him

in a way that had nothing to do with rage or retribution. He exhaled sharply.

'Vieri!' She backed further into the pillows.

'I'm sorry, Harper, I couldn't stop him.' Leah was in the doorway behind him.

'That's okay, Leah. You can go.'

'I'm not going to leave you.'

'Please, Leah.'

'You heard what she said.' Speaking over his shoulder, Vieri's chilling tone could not be disobeyed. As Leah shut the door he jammed his hands into his coat pockets and for a long moment he and Harper stared at one another. Vieri could feel the muscle twitching along his jaw.

'So…' Finally Harper broke the silence. 'What are you doing here, Vieri?'

'You can cut the pretence.' Vieri advanced towards the bed. 'Leah has told me.'

'Ah.'

'*Si*, ah.'

'Look, Vieri, I know I should have said something before but…'

'But what, Harper?'

'But I needed to sort things out in my head first.'

'So that's what you call it, is it? Sorting things out?'

Harper stared back at him. She had expected shock, anger maybe, but not directed at her, and not like this. His whole body was taut with cold fury, as if his rage had solidified the very bones of him.

Pulling back the covers, she got out of bed and, in a futile attempt to stand up to him, placed herself squarely before him. So close now, she could feel the heat of his temper, almost smell it on his skin. Never had she seen him like this before.

'Look.' She reached out to touch his arm but he recoiled in horror. 'This has obviously come as a shock to you, but maybe if we could just sit down calmly and talk it through…?'

'It's a little late for that, Harper.' His voice leeched scorn. 'I'm sure you think you have fixed this problem, the way you fix everyone and everything else in your life. But believe me, Harper, there is no fixing me.'

'I'm sorry you feel like that, Vieri.' She pushed the hair away from her face, still trying to inject some calm, soothe his rabid temper. 'But if it makes you feel better, I am prepared to take full responsibility.'

'Better?' He cursed violently in Sicilian, reaching towards her with a hand that shook with emotion before changing his mind and shoving it back into his pocket, as if he couldn't bring himself to touch her. 'You think your taking *full responsibility* is going to make me feel better? Are you mad, woman?'

Harper stared at him aghast. If she was to question anyone's sanity, it would be his. His rage had turned him from the cool, controlled man that she thought she'd known into some sort of raving beast. She wouldn't have been surprised to see him foam at the mouth. Never had she seen this side of him before, never had she expected him to react like this, as if it were all her fault. And yet still she knew she loved him. Still her heart melted at the sight of him.

'Why are you behaving like this?' She wanted to reach out to touch him so badly, but instead she folded her arms across her chest.

'And tell me, Harper, how exactly am I supposed to behave? How should a man appear on learning that his…his wife has made a unilateral decision to end her pregnancy?'

'What?' She stared at him, shock and confusion knotting her brow, dulling her brain.

'You heard.'

'You…you think that I have had an abortion?'

'Don't insult my intelligence by trying to deny it. Leah has told me the truth.'

'No, Vieri, she hasn't.' Now she reached for his shoulders, her hands shaking with raw emotion. 'Or at least, whatever she has told you, you have misunderstood.'

Vieri felt Harper's slim hands on his coat, fluttering like a trapped bird. And this time he didn't try and shrug them off. Standing there in her sensible pyjamas, her tawny eyes wide, imploring, she looked so adorable, so vulnerable. He rapidly searched her face for clues. He saw confusion and hurt, but not guilt. Had he got this wrong? Instantly another terrible thought flashed through his mind. What if she had lost the baby, suffered a miscarriage?

'Harper?' He cupped her face in his hands, staring deep into her eyes. 'Tell me now. What have I misunderstood?'

'I haven't got rid of our baby, Vieri.' Her eyes held his. 'I would never do such a thing.'

Our baby. Vieri briefly closed his eyes against the painful wonder of that word.

'So, what, then? You have had a miscarriage?' The words felt like boulders in his throat.

'No.' Harper shook her head beneath his grasp, her hands leaving his shoulders to rest on her stomach. 'I thought that was what was happening when I woke up this morning with stomach pains but I went to see the doctor and she said—'

'You are still pregnant?' With a leap of hope, Vieri tilted her face so he would finally see the truth. And what he saw melted his heart.

'Yes.' Fat tears leaked from her eyes. 'Yes, I am.'

'Grazie Dio!' He pulled her against him, crushing her in his arms. Relief flooded through him,

hot and heady, stirring up other emotions in its wake. Joy, hope, *love*.

Harper let him hold her, her body moulding against his, wonderfully soft and responsive to his embrace. But then the moment passed and she stiffened, moving against him. 'You are pleased?' She muffled the words against his coat, then pushed herself away to look up into his face.

'*Si, certo*, of course.' But at the sight of her anxious face Vieri's fears crept in again. 'What exactly did the doctor say?'

'She said that I should rest and if the spasms stop and I don't get any more then everything should be okay.' She sniffed, brushing away the tears with the back of her hand. 'She has booked me in for a scan in a couple of days.'

'And have they stopped, the pains?'

Harper nodded, but she had to bite down on her lip before she could meet his eyes. 'I haven't had any for several hours now.'

'So that it good, *si*?' Relief flooded his voice.

'Yes, it's good.' She gave him a watery smile. Of course it was good; it was more than good. But having Vieri here, standing in her bedroom looking ridiculously out of place in his dark coat, seeming even taller than usual beneath the low ceiling, had brought another pain that was nothing to do with her pregnancy. She loved him so much. Seeing him again, after several weeks' absence, only made her realise it more.

'You should get back into bed.' Suddenly Vieri was swooping her up into his arms and carrying her over to the bed, where he pulled back the duvet and settled her underneath. 'There.' He tenderly brushed the hair back from her forehead. 'You must rest.'

Fat chance of that. As Harper gazed at him, every nerve ending in her body tingled with awareness, every cell longed for him, yearned for him. But she knew she had to be strong, be sensible.

Vieri's extreme reaction to the pregnancy had shocked her. His anger when he had thought she'd had a termination was perhaps understandable, although she suspected there were many men who would have greeted that news with relief. But Vieri wasn't like other men. He was proud and he was strong and just the sight of him filled her heart to overflowing. But he wasn't hers. And even though now he knew the truth his attitude had dramatically changed and he appeared to be so happy about the baby, thrilled even, that didn't mean that anything had changed. In terms of what they were going to do now, how they would raise the child, how she would cope with the agony of loving a man who didn't love her back, she had no idea.

One step at a time, she decided, arranging the duvet around her. Somehow they would make it work. They had to.

'So what are you actually doing here, Vieri?' She delved down into her shallow reserves of reason to try and sound normal. 'You didn't think to tell me you were coming?'

'It was a spur-of-the-moment thing.' Vieri shrugged off his coat and pulled up a chair, positioning it by the bed.

'Can I ask why?'

'I wanted to see you.' He made it sound like the most natural thing in the world, especially when he took hold of her hand that lay outside the covers and laced his fingers through hers. 'Though it was never my intention to come storming in like a wild beast. I'm so sorry.'

'That's okay. You were upset.'

'No, it's not okay. It was unforgivable. Especially when you are supposed to be getting peace and rest.'

'There's no harm done.' She gave him a reassuring smile.

'Thankfully not.' He gave her a solemn stare. 'But I owe you an explanation.'

'No, really, there's no need…'

Raising a finger, he pressed it against her lips to silence her.

'Yes, Harper, there is. There is something I

need to tell you.' He hesitated and Harper could see the internal struggle playing across his face, as if he was waging war with himself. 'Many years ago I fathered another child.' He watched her intently, searching for her reaction. 'I was eighteen. I thought she was the love of my life, but it turned out I was wrong.'

'Oh, Vieri.' Harper gripped his hand more tightly.

'She had an abortion without even telling me she was pregnant. I only found out by chance afterwards.'

'I'm so sorry.' Suddenly realisation dawned. 'And you thought I'd done the same thing?'

Vieri shrugged his apology. 'Stupid, I know. I just jumped to the wrong conclusion. Forgive me, Harper.'

'There's nothing to forgive. This girl obviously hurt you very much.'

'That's just it—she wasn't a girl. She was a woman.' He hesitated again, before dragging in a deep breath. 'It was Donatella Sorrentino.'

Donatella Sorrentino. Harper felt the pain of her name spear through her. She should have known. The woman whose dark presence had always been swirling around in the background. Who Harper had long suspected meant more to Vieri than he had ever admitted. Now she knew the truth.

She pulled her hand away from his clasp.

'And you still love her?' Her voice sounded very small.

'No!' Vieri's reply was immediate, vehement. Too vehement. 'Whatever makes you think that?'

Harper looked down at the bedclothes, unable to meet his gaze, frightened of what she might see there.

'Because I saw the way you reacted when I told you she had chosen my dress for the ball. And again at Castello di Trevente after Alfonso died. Both times you behaved like a man possessed...' she picked at the duvet cover '...or a man in love.'

'No!' Vieri could only repeat the word in astonishment. He gazed at Harper's bent head, at the soft auburn curls falling to cover her face. How could she have got this so wrong? How could she have misunderstood him so completely? But then it was hardly surprising when he thought of the way he had treated her. All the harassment and bullying, using her for his own gain, or, even worse, his own satisfaction. Forcing her to marry him and then banishing her from the *castello* before turning up here hollering like a raving lunatic. It was no wonder Harper jumped to wrong conclusions, thought so badly of him, had no real measure of who he was. Who could blame her?

Shame coursed through him, hot and strong.

He had to try and put things right. It was time to come out of the murky shadows and be honest with Harper, show her the man he really was. Except he was no longer sure who that man was.

A few months ago it would have been easy. Hugely successful billionaire businessman with a formidable reputation for working hard and for enjoying the fruits of his success. A man at the top of his game, always in control, a man who had taken on the world and won. Invincible, ruthless, *heartless*.

But now…now as Harper slowly raised her head to look at him again and he caught sight of her beautiful face, he realised that none of that material success mattered. None of it actually meant anything. His whole life had been a hollow shell…until now.

Getting to his feet, he moved over to the window, trying to order his thoughts, make some sense of this astonishing shift in his values. But first things first—he had to put Harper right about Donatella. Drawing in a breath, he turned to face her again. 'I promise you, Harper, any love I may have felt for Donatella died a very long time ago. Now all I feel is anger. That's what you have witnessed.'

'But so much anger?' She refused to let go. 'And after all these years? Surely time should have allowed you to put it behind you, move on.'

She was right, of course. He had carried this hatred for Donatella for far too long. So long that it had become part of who he was, almost as if letting go of it would be losing a chunk of himself. It had become his own personal vendetta. And deep down he knew why. Not just because Donatella had betrayed the Calleroni family, the callous way she had as good as signed her own father's death warrant and broken Alfonso's heart. Not the vile way she had groomed him on the orders of the Sorrentino family, used him and then dumped him. Not even the actual act of the abortion. His problem was more basic than that, more fundamental. He had never analysed the root cause before—he had never needed to. But suddenly he wanted Harper to understand.

Moving towards the end of the bed, he gripped the iron railing, the metal cold against his hot hands.

'I know how important family is to you, Harper. I have seen the way you care for your loved ones.' He started slowly, trying to keep his voice level, neutral, aiming for facts rather than emotion. 'And despite the impression I may have given you, I really admire you for that.'

Harper stared at him, waiting.

'But I grew up without a family. Apart from Alfonso, I had no one to show me any love, or to love in return.'

'That's so sad.' Her soft, gentle voice immediately pulled at the threads of his composure. Vieri shrugged.

'I never really knew any different. But when Donatello had that abortion, she terminated my only known blood relative. That was why my reaction was so extreme.' He swallowed hard. 'With that one, selfish act, she denied me the possibility of a family of my own. Someone to care for, for the first time.'

'Oh, Vieri.' Pulling back the covers, Harper scrambled to the end of the bed, kneeling before him and placing her hands over his clasped fists.

'And I believe that is the reason I have found it so hard to let it go.' He pushed on to the end, determined to be honest with himself—with her.

'Of course. I understand completely.' Reaching up, Harper touched his cheek with the back of her hand, a gesture so gentle, so simple, but so right. Vieri felt his heart melt. 'And all those emotions were stirred up again when you thought I had done the same thing.'

'No.' For the first time Vieri realised that wasn't true. He reached for her hand. 'No, this is different. The reason I reacted so violently when I thought you had had an abortion is because...' he hesitated, discovering the truth as he spoke the words '...because I want this baby. So very much.'

'I see.' Harper withdrew her hand and sat back on her heels, a wariness creeping into her voice.

'No, you don't.' He moved to the side of the bed. 'This has nothing to do with my childhood or what Donatella did or the family I have never had. It is simply because this baby is ours, Harper, yours and mine. That's what makes it so special.'

'Well, thank you for sharing that with me.' She turned her head away, as if unwilling or unable to process his words.

'It is I who should be thanking you.' Suddenly Vieri realised how true that was. Catching hold of her chin, he turned her to face him again, searching deep into her eyes. Beneath the vulnerability he could see such tenderness, such compassion that something shifted inside him. Like a beam of light shining through the gloom of his past existence, he realised that the anger that had been with him so long had lifted, gone, miraculously evaporated. Donatella meant nothing to him any more. *And Harper everything.*

But still he hesitated, still he tried to hold back the surge of emotions that was straining to break free. He had to think about Harper now, what was best for her. The cruel way he had treated her in the past tormented him, but he had always been so sure it had been for her own good. To protect her from the man he was—from his blackened heart. A heart that had been so badly damaged all those years ago that it had petrified inside him, like a chunk of fossilised wood. But now as he looked into those remarkable autumn-coloured eyes he realised he had been wrong all along. His heart hadn't been irretrievably damaged after all. He had just never come across anyone to breathe life into it. Until now.

Outside the rain was coming down heavily, the wind lashing it against the small window, darkening the room. Taking hold of Harper's hands, Vieri solemnly held them before him.

'I have so much to thank you for, Harper.' He spoke quietly, feeling his way, his voice competing with the sound of the rain. 'You are the most remarkable, beautiful, caring woman I have ever met. But it is time for someone to take care of you. I am that person. From now on I am going to look after you, you and the baby. I promise you, you will want for nothing.'

Harper held herself very still. She could see the sincerity in his eyes, feel it in his voice, almost believe that, for once, she was all that mattered. *Almost.* She gave her head a small shake. 'You don't need to do that.'

'Oh, but I do, *cara*. More than you could possibly know.' He stroked the palms of her hands with his thumbs. 'From now on you and our unborn child are all that I care about. Your happiness is everything to me.'

'Vieri… I…' Harper pulled away her hands and, slipping off the bed, came and stood before him. Vieri could see her bottom lip staring to quiver, hear the threat of tears in her voice.

'Please, Harper,' he quickly tried to intercept. 'Let me do this. I know that you have every right to hate me after the way I have treated you but let me try and make it up to you.'

'That's just it, Vieri. I don't hate you.' Now the tears were starting to fall, silently rolling down her cheek. 'I could never hate you. I almost wish I did.'

'But why?' He frowned down at her anguished face, uncomprehending.

'Because to hate you would be much easier.' She took in a short, brave breath. 'Loving you is the hard thing.'

There, she had said it. Like stepping off a cliff, Harper felt herself go into freefall, the world spinning around her. By opening up to her, Vieri had released her to say the thing that had been haunting her for so long. And to her surprise she felt a profound sense of release. A calm sense of 'what will be, will be'. *Que sera sera.*

'What are you saying, *cara*?' Vieri leant in, searching her eyes for answers.

'I'm saying that I love you, Vieri. With all my heart.'

With tears still blocking her throat, she waited

as Vieri took in this information, refusing to let herself try and analyse the fleeting expressions of shock and surprise that were flitting across the face that she loved so much. Finally, silently, he wrapped his arms around her, pulling her into a tight embrace.

'But why do you cry, *cara*?' He breathed into the tangle of her hair.

'Because I never meant for this to happen.' Buried against his shoulder, Harper felt the torrent of words begin to tumble from her mouth. 'And I know you don't feel the same way and that's fine because we will still be good parents and raise our child together and I don't expect anything from you, romantically I mean, because I know you couldn't give that and...'

'Harper!'

'...and I would certainly hate you to think that you had to stay with me out of some sort of pity. That would be awful and totally unacceptable, of course.'

'Harper, stop!' Pulling away, he gazed into her face. 'Let me speak. I need to tell you something. I need to make you see what is here, in my heart.' He spread his hand across his chest. 'You mean everything to me, Harper, *everything*. With or without the baby, you are the centre of my world. My world would have no meaning without you in it.'

A delirious sensation flooded through her, weakening her bones, stealing all words. But Vieri hadn't finished yet.

Brushing a strand of hair away from her heated face, he held her gaze with an intensity that permeated her very soul. 'Because I love you, Harper. With my whole being. With everything I have to give.'

'You do?' Her eyes were bright with shock.

'I do. And I am only sorry that it has taken me this long to realise.' Clasping her hands, he poured out his confession, determined that she should see it, *feel it*. 'Now I know the truth I realise it has been there all along. I love you, Harper, and I want to spend the rest of my life with you. That's if you will have me, of course.'

'Oh, Vieri!' With a certainty that set her heart alight, she realised it was true. He really did love her. Every bit as much as she loved him.

His lips came down on hers, softly at first, but immediately deepening as the ecstasy took hold, the heat of their love spreading between them until they melded together as one. Until they were kissing, not just with their mouths but with their breath and their blood, their hearts and their souls. All that they were.

'Can I take that as a yes?' Pausing for a second for them to catch their breath, Vieri pulled back to gaze down at her.

'Yes, Vieri.' She tipped her chin, her eyes shining. 'You can.'

'*Mille grazie, mio amore.* I can't tell you what that means to me.' He brushed her lips again. 'I'm just wondering...' He looked over her shoulder. 'D'you think there is room in that bed for two?'

With a wide smile, Harper took his hand. 'Don't you mean three?'

'I do, don't I?' Vieri stared at her, shaking his head in amazement. 'You and the baby—I have to be the luckiest man alive.'

Outside the window the rain had stopped and a brilliant rainbow arced across the sky. Whether it was in agreement or celebration or merely a meteorological coincidence didn't really matter. Snuggled up in bed, lost in the wonder of their joy and very, very much in love, Vieri and Harper knew that, no matter what, their happiness would last for ever.

EPILOGUE

'WE ARE HERE, *mio figlio*.' Bringing the car gently to a halt outside the *castello*, Vieri turned to look at his precious cargo. His wife, Harper, and beside her, asleep in his car seat, his newborn son. 'Welcome to Castello di Trevente.' Harper smiled back at him and Vieri's heart swelled with tenderness and love.

Being there as his wife gave birth to their child had been the most exhilarating, terrifying, astonishing experience of his life. The labour had been long and seeing Harper in pain hard to endure and at times his concern for her had almost got the better of him. Only Harper's calm insistence that she was in control had stopped him from roaring down the corridors to demand somebody did something, or summonsing every medic in the land to come to her aid if necessary.

But in the end his beautiful, brave Harper had done it all on her own, with just the help of the midwife, who had made it clear she had no time for Vieri's histrionics. Seeing his son take his first lungful of air, then lovingly held against Harper's chest, had all but undone him, the whole miracle of life almost too much to take in. And when the baby had been wrapped in a towel and handed to him, when he had gazed into his son's deep blue eyes for the first time, the full swell of emotion had taken over. And Vieri had done nothing to try to hide it.

Now, only twenty-four hours later, here they were, back at Castello di Trevente. And their life together as a family could finally begin.

'Here, let me.' Opening the car door, he helped his wife out, then went round to unbuckle the baby's car seat. Coming beside him, Harper slipped her arm through his and together the three of them ascended the steps to the entrance.

'Wait a minute.' Putting down the car seat, Vieri lifted out the baby and, cradling him in the crook of one arm, clasped Harper's hand with the other. 'There, that's better. Alfie needs to have a better view of his new home. Look, Harper, he's opened his eyes.'

It was true, he had. And as Harper gazed at her baby son cradled in Vieri's arm she thought she might burst with happiness.

The housekeeper opened the door, duly fussing over the baby as if he was the most remarkable infant in the world, which clearly he was. Going into the salon, they settled themselves on the sofa as she bustled off to bring them some refreshments.

Harper looked around her, at her husband, her son, at the beautiful room they were now in, still having to pinch herself that it was real. Discovering that Alfonso had left them Castello di Trevente as a wedding present had been the most wonderful surprise. They had been living here for a couple of months now, and, although in some ways it still felt like a dream, it was also starting to feel like home. The whole place had been beautifully refurbished, a project that Harper had loved overseeing during her pregnancy, apart from when Vieri was fussing over her and insisting that she was doing too much. Now it was the most amazing for ever home that Alfonso had wanted for them. All the more so since baby Alfie had joined them.

'Are you comfortable? Can I get you anything?' Slipping one arm around her shoulder, the other still holding Alfie, Vieri pulled her close.

'No, I'm fine.' She reached for his hand, threading her fingers through his. 'In fact, everything is perfect.'

'It is, isn't it?' Leaning in, Vieri kissed her softly on the lips. Alfie, pressed between them, gave a small grunt of disapproval.

'Though we had better make the most of the peace and quiet.' Harper pulled a mirthful face.

'We've got Leah and my father descending on us tomorrow.'

'Don't remind me!' Vieri looked down tenderly at his son. 'Don't worry, *figlio*, I will protect you from your mad auntie Leah.'

Harper laughed. 'She's just excited, that's all.' It was true that Leah's constant calls as she had waited for news of the birth had been a bit over the top, eventually leading to Vieri insisting they turned off their mobile phones. But, of course, she had been the first one Harper had called when Alfie had finally arrived—Harper's eardrums were still recovering from her shrieks of joy. 'I'm so glad Dad has agreed to come with her.'

'Me too.' Running the palm of his hand over Alfie's soft, downy head, he addressed his son. 'From now on we guys have to stick together.' He looked back at Harper. 'I have to say I like your father. I think we are going to get on fine.'

'He is a good man. It was just that after Mum died he lost his way.'

'Grief can do strange things to a man.'

'Indeed.' They locked eyes, Vieri acknowledging Harper's knowing look with a wry smile. 'And the project you have involved him in has given him a new lease of life. He's a changed man. Thank you so much for that.'

'*Nessun problema.* Your father has such a wealth of knowledge and I intend to exploit that to the full while he's here. I have set up meetings with a couple of my land managers to see about starting to keep game birds on some of the estates. It could turn into a lucrative business. I'd happily employ Angus full time if he'd let me.'

'Dad's roots are in Scotland and the Craigmore estate is his life's work. You will never persuade him to leave. Leah, on the other hand…'

'No-o-o.' Covering Alfie's small ears with his strong hands, Vieri recoiled in mock horror. 'We didn't hear that, did we, Alfie?'

Laughing, Harper gave him a playful punch on the arm and Vieri pulled her in for another kiss. 'I don't mean it. Your family is my family now. And I have to say, that feels surprisingly good. Plus, of course…' he gave her a cheeky grin '… I am very much looking forward to increasing its numbers. I think it is our duty to provide lots of brothers and sisters for Alfie.'

'Our duty, eh?' She raised her eyebrows at him.

'There may be some pleasure involved along the way.'

Harper laughed again, knowing for certain that there would.

'And to think this is all down to Alfonso.' She offered her finger to Alfie, who took it in his tiny grasp. 'We have so much to thank him for.'

'We do indeed.'

'I hope he would approve of what we've done

with the *castello*.' She glanced around her. 'It looks very different from when he lived here.'

'Believe me, Alfonso won't be worrying about the decorations. He'll be too busy gloating over the way his plan has come together. I bet he's looking down feeling thoroughly pleased with himself.'

'You think?'

'I know. And his spirit will always be here at Castello di Trevente. He is part of the fabric of the place.'

'That's true. And of course his name will live on in this little one.'

'So it will.'

Kissing the top of his son's head, Vieri turned to his wife. 'And together, my most beautiful Harper, I know we will make him proud. The future starts here, *amore mio*, with you, me and baby Alfie. And it is going to be the most wonderful future ever!'

* * * * *